I0708322

The ENLIGHTENMENT

A Magical Tale

A Novel By

Victoria Raikel

This book is dedicated to all of humanity, to the animals that roam the land, to the birds that soar through the skies, to the beautiful flowers and majestic trees, to our wondrous oceans full of life, and to all living things on Earth. We must cherish what we are given as together we possess the power to change the world and preserve this splendor for generations to come.

Let's create a world where

magic thrives, nature flourishes,

and our planet finds harmony once more.

With magical dust,

boundless imagination,

and a heart for conservation. 🧡

~Victoria Raikel

H ELLO, MY NAME IS EMILIE, AND I AM HERE TO TELL you a story that involves magic; beautiful, mysterious creatures from the land and sea; and saving your world—that is, the human world, Earth.

This is a story that everyone should read. It tells of how only nine days and one person can change your world into a better place. And, I ask you, if one person can make such a dramatic change for the better, can you imagine what ten, one hundred, or one thousand people could do? I mean, I was told you had about eight billion humans on Earth, so surely your planet could produce ten people like Tom.

Who is Tom? you ask. *And what did he do that was so great?*

Well, you must read on to find out!

The story takes place in the magical land of Azar. Azar exists on a different dimension than your world. Azar has its own universe, star system, moon, sun, and planets. No one knows how long it has been in existence, but I am 9,737 years old, and there are other creatures that are much older. Many different creatures live on Azar. They can talk and fly, and they have superior strength and magical powers.

Now, about me. I am a pixie with beautiful blue, iridescent wings. I'm highly intelligent and have magical powers that would blow your mind. My friends tell me that I'm very strong because I can lift two giant dragons above my head with one hand and throw them a couple miles away, which they seem to like very much.

My interest in your planet Earth all began around eight hundred years ago, when we started getting "visitors" from other planets. They would appear out of nowhere, and we would see them walking in the forests or on the beaches. Theodore the Owl, who is one of our wisest creatures on Azar, determined that there was a portal that would open to other worlds a few times a century, and he could tell what day a visitor would arrive by the alignment of the stars. The portal would open for a visitor to come through and then re-open again in nine days so the visitor could go back to where they'd come from. At first, this happened every thirty years, but for the past four hundred years, it has been occurring more frequently. Theodore does not know why this phenomenon happens, but he is a very smart owl, and he will find the reason why.

So, all of us Azarians have adapted to visitors from other worlds, and sometimes it's great getting to know different cultures and customs, but sometimes it can be very troublesome.

In a couple days, we will have a visitor from another world and here is where the story begins…

TWO DAYS BEFORE THE ARRIVAL

T HE MIGHTY GREEN DRAGON ROCKETED THROUGH the sky above the cliffs of Azar, performing spectacular aerobatic maneuvers. He dove straight down, spun upward at a dizzying rate, and did three-hundred-sixty-degree rolls through the air with ease. He looped in circles, picking up momentum, and shot straight into the sky at lightning speed. He was doing the glorious "D-Bomb" maneuver, aka the Dragon Bomb, where he looped around, gradually picking up speed, shot straight up at full throttle, then disappeared in the blink of an eye.

His name was Dracodian or "Cody" for short. He was considered one of the fastest creatures on Azar. Tomorrow was the Moon Races, where he would be competing with other creatures for the title of

"The Fastest Creature on Azar." He'd trained for the event every morning for the last three months, and it was definitely paying off, as his top speed was clocked at ten thousand mph, or thirteen times the speed of sound, which by far beats Earth's fastest jet-powered aircraft going at seven thousand mph.

After an hour of diligent practicing, Cody grew tired and flew home, where he lived with his family atop the cliffs overlooking Azar's beautiful turquoise waters and white sand beaches. The Dragon family consisted of Georgina the mother, who was a red dragon, Archibald aka Archie the father, who was a blue dragon, and their son Cody, who was a green dragon. Georgina was busy baking up a storm and brewing her secret recipe of dragon beer and other exotic drinks that she would serve to the thirsty and hungry Azarians at the races tomorrow.

There was a knock on the door, and outside stood Emilie the pixie and Nala the white tiger, two of Cody's best friends. Nala was a majestic white tiger with black stripes. He had striking blue eyes and magnificent, elegant wings with which to fly. He was enormous when standing on all four legs at a height of eight feet tall. He could run at lightning speed and had the strength of a hundred elephants put together.

Emilie was a beautiful pixie with blue, iridescent wings. She stood six feet tall and had light brown hair that hung below her shoulders, hazel-brown eyes, and an olive complexion. She was a very sweet and charming pixie and also one of the most powerful creatures on Azar. She could move giant boulders and throw humongous dragons with one hand a staggering distance. She was also highly intelligent, speaking more than ten thousand languages, including many that were spoken on Earth. Nala and Emilie lived together in a cozy cottage located in the Enchanted Forest where Cody often visited.

These three best friends had been chosen to be the "welcoming committee" for visitors who crossed through the portal. They were tasked with welcoming the visitor from day one and showing them the stunning sights of Azar for the nine-day period of their stay. They were to protect the visitor from harm and also protect Azar from the visitor if need be.

Emilie was first chosen because she was the creature that looked most like humans, as the majority of the visitors were from Earth. They felt more comfortable communicating with someone that looked like them. Nala and Cody came along in case the visitor didn't behave, as many of them didn't acclimate well in the first couple days and tried to do foolish things. Nala and Cody also helped with the care and transportation of the visitor to various places around Azar.

Emilie, Nala, and Cody got very good at being the welcoming committee and had a routine for dealing with the visitors that worked rather well. They enjoyed it, as they learned a lot about different cultures and customs that they and all of Azar incorporated into their daily lives.

Archie opened the door and said, "Why, it's Emilie and Nala here for you, Cody. Come in, guys!"

They walked in and saw Georgina hard at work brewing her secret batch.

Emilie said, "Do you need some help?"

Georgina said, "That's sweet of you, but Archie and I are almost done. Cody just finished his morning practice session and will be out in a minute. Why don't you and Nala sit down and have some freshly baked dragonberry pie?"

Cody walked in and was happy to see his two best friends. Nala said, "We saw you do the D-Bomb earlier, and that was faster than yesterday's time. You're gonna smoke the competition away, Cody!"

They had all sat down and were discussing tomorrow's race when Archie looked out the window and said, "It looks like we have another visitor. It's Theodore the Owl."

Theodore was known as a "Great Owl," which was considered one of the most esteemed positions amongst the Azarians. A Great Owl was knowledgeable in all fields of arts and science. He was a navigator of the stars and was looked up to by all creatures of Azar. Theodore stood at four feet tall and had a wing span of twelve feet wide. His feathers were medium brown in color and light brown around his face. He had big black eyes and sharp talons that hung from his feet. He wore a brilliant emerald green stone that hung from his neck. Theodore served on the Council that oversaw the safety and care of the visitors from other worlds. The Council was made up of three of the wisest and respected creatures on Azar.

Theodore flew in and landed on the porch. He caught a good whiff of the baking and said, "Mmmm mmmm, that smells delicious! Looks like I came just in time."

Cody walked out with a tray of freshly baked pie, a couple

mugs of dragon beer and a pitcher of Dragon's Delight, which was a mixture of dragonberries, dragonfruit, coconut, and other exotic fruits. Dragon's Delight was Theodore's favorite drink. They all sat on the porch, had refreshments, and spoke about the big race tomorrow.

Archie said, "So, Theodore, how many contestants are in the Moon Race?"

Theodore said, "There are ten, and it looks like it's going to be a good one!"

Georgina said, "Cody has been practicing hard every day, and he's gonna win!"

Everyone nodded in agreement.

Archie raised his mug and said, "To Cody, the fastest creature on Azar!"

They all raised their glasses and said, "To Cody!"

Theodore finished his pie and said to Emilie, Nala, and Cody, "I need to speak with you all about an important matter."

They nodded, got up, and walked toward the edge of the cliff.

Theodore said, "We have a visitor arriving in two days."

Emilie said, "Is it that time already? It's been twenty-five years?"

Theodore said, "It's been twenty years since our last visitor. I'm afraid it is opening sooner than expected. I looked at the stars yesterday, and they will align in two days. The portal will open over Azar's waters."

Nala said, "Then we must inform the mermaids of Meridien. They will need to be on alert for the visitor."

Meridien was a kingdom of mermaids and sea creatures that lived in the waters of Azar. Oriana the Mermaid was the queen of Meridien.

Theodore said, "I'm on my way there to speak with Oriana after I finish up here. They will be ready."

Emilie said, "And we'll be ready for the visitor."

Theodore said his goodbyes to everyone and flew over Azar's waters to inform the Kingdom of Meridien the visitor was coming.

ONE DAY BEFORE THE ARRIVAL —THE MOON RACES

THE TRUMPETS SOUNDED OFF THE START OF THE festivities. The Moon Race started at Azar's Grandstand at precisely 7 p.m., when the moon was up and shining. Georgina and Archie manned the refreshment booth as creatures lined up to get a taste of the freshly baked morsels and have a mug of their favorite drinks. Creatures played games and danced to their favorite tunes.

Sammy the Mushroom of The Mushroom Band announced that the next song would be the "Electric Moon Rap" and asked all creatures to come to center stage and do the Moon Dance. The Mushroom Band consisted of three members. Dewey was in charge of the DJ booth and keyboards, Louie was on guitar, and Sammy was the lead singer. They were extremely large mushrooms that stood five feet tall. They had skinny, long arms and fingers, long stems, and short legs with feet. They had big red mushroom caps with white spots and wore sunglasses. Sammy Mushroom was the star of the show, as he could sing, dance, and even rap, and the "Electric Moon Rap" showed off his skills.

Everyone lined up in rows and got ready. Dewey started playing a hip-hop beat, and Louie started beatboxing into the microphone. Sammy took center stage and started rapping:

"Now all you funky creatures out there
Throw your hands up, and wave them in the air
Listen to me and follow my instructions
My name is Sammy Mushroom of the
Mushroom Band Production."

"Come on, everyone, now get on your feet
Do the Moon Dance, and dance to the beat.
Two steps to the left, two steps to the right
Do the funky walk and dance all night!

Now let's shimmy shimmy up and shimmy shimmy down
Do the touchdown all the way to the ground
Get on your head and spin yourself around
That's it, Azarians! Now let's take it to town!"

The Azarians danced with electric, robotic moves, spun on their heads, and did the Moon Dance. The song concluded, and everyone clapped and cheered. The Mushroom Band took a bow and played their next song.

Meanwhile, Emilie and Nala arrived to cheer on Cody. They saw him stretching and preparing for the race alongside the other contestants. They walked over, and Emilie said, "How you doing, Cody?"

Cody said, "Nervous. I'm almost done warming up. It looks like I have some tough competition. Zania the Empress Cat and Dillon the Red Phoenix are pretty fast."

Emilie said, "Come on, Cody, you got this! You're the fastest creature here, and you know it. Now focus and do your best!"

Cody took a deep breath and said, "Okay, I'm ready—let's do it!"

The trumpeters alerted everyone it was time for the main event. The contestants approached the starting line and were ready to go.

The Moon beamed a light down on the creatures and in a deep

and thunderous voice said, "Hello, fellow Azarians, and welcome to the Annual Moon Races. Now, the first creature that reaches me will be the winner and crowned 'The Fastest Creature on Azar!' Runners, get on your mark! …Get ready! …Get set! …GO!"

And they were off! Dillon the Red Phoenix was in the lead, followed by Zania the Empress Cat, and Cody was third. The other contestants trailed far behind the three front runners. At the halfway point, Cody steamed ahead of Zania and closed the gap between Dillon and himself. Everyone cheered them on, as it was now between Cody and Dillon, who were neck and neck.

Cody knew he had to make a move. He took a deep breath, gave it all his might, zipped past Dillon, took the lead, and won!

The Moon shouted out to everyone down in Azar, "Cody is the winner! Cody is the winner!"

The Azarians rejoiced and chanted, "Cody! Cody! Cody!"

Cody was ecstatic! He jumped up and down in the air and looped around the Moon at bullet speed.

The Moon said, "Congratulations, Cody, you pulled out a fast one at the end! Good job, my friend. All of Azar is waiting to celebrate with you. Go have some fun!"

Cody gave the Moon a thumbs up then raced back to Azar. Everyone celebrated and congratulated him on his triumph. Georgina and Archie crowned him with a beautiful floral wreath. Archie carried his son on his shoulders and paraded him around the grandstand.

Theodore presented him with a big, shiny trophy and said, "Congratulations to Cody, who is the winner and champion of this year's Moon Race!" The giant trophy shined brilliant gold and was inscribed "The Fastest Creature on Azar—Cody the Dragon."

Everyone clapped and jumped up and down and chanted with excitement, "Cody! Cody! Cody! Cody!"

The Mushroom Band started to play upbeat music, and all of Azar danced and celebrated throughout the night.

DAY 1
THE ARRIVAL

I T WAS MORNING IN THE ENCHANTED FOREST, AND Emilie and Nala were fast asleep after a night of celebration. There was a knock on the door, and Emilie woke up to see who it was.

Emilie's room was nice and cozy. It had a large four-poster bed made of old branches. It was dressed with vines of leaves and small blue flowers that wrapped around the canopy and draped along the posts and edges of the bed. The bed was filled with large, soft, green leaves, and a light blue, fluffy blanket and pillow lay on top. There was a mirror and dresser in the corner that also had vines of blue flowers hanging down each side, and a rocking chair sat by the window that overlooked a garden. In the far-left corner was a closet full of clothes and shoes.

Emilie got up and went to the kitchen, as she heard a tapping noise at the kitchen door. Emilie yawned and said, "It's probably Cody." She opened the door, and it was Cody with a table full of food and drinks.

Cody said, "Good morning! I brought you some breakfast. Is Nala still asleep? We have a big day ahead of us!"

Nala appeared and said, "Good morning, everyone." He walked straight to the table outside, tied a napkin around his neck, and started digging in.

Emilie and Cody sat down as well. They were famished after a night of dancing and celebration and ate quickly. They spoke about the festivities last night and Cody's exciting win. Cody still couldn't believe that he was "The Fastest Creature on Azar," but he was all smiles and ready for the adventure that awaited them.

Emilie said, "Well, we better get going. Our visitor will be here soon."

They got ready and flew to the beaches of Azar.

They landed at the cliffs and could see Georgina and Archie with other creatures looking down toward the beach area. They approached the edge of the cliff, looked down, and saw the mermaids on shore surrounding a body laid out on the sand.

There were six mermaids mounted on giant seahorses encircling the body. Oriana the Mermaid looked up and waved them down. The three of them flew to the shore and saw the body up close.

Oriana said, "We found the visitor lying face down on the rocks at Red Point about thirty minutes ago. It was unconscious, so we brought it straight here. It looks human to me."

Emilie approached the visitor. It was a human man. He was dressed in a business suit that was torn and muddied. He had dark brown, short hair; light skin; and was tall and slim.

Nala asked, "Is he dead?"

Emilie said, "No, he's not dead. He's breathing."

Emilie tried to wake the human. She slapped his cheeks a few times and pinched his nose…nothing. Emilie said to Oriana, "Can you splash some water on the human?"

The giant seahorse splashed a great deal of water on him with his tail.

It worked. The human started to choke and gasp for air. Emilie quickly sat him up and tapped his back to help him. He stopped choking then took a deep breath. He looked up at the sun beating upon him and squinted. He was dazed and confused, trying to make sense of what was happening. Then he heard a women's voice next to him. He turned toward the voice and could barely make out what was next to him, as everything was a blur.

Emilie said, "Hello. My name is Emilie. Are you okay?"

He rubbed his eyes and opened them again. He could see Emilie's face more clearly. He said, "Where am I? Who are you?"

Emilie said, "My name is Emilie, what is your name?"

He looked down at his torn and wet clothes and answered, "Tom, my name is Tom. Where am I? What happened to my clothes? I'm all wet."

Emilie said, "Listen, Tom, I will explain to you what happened, but you must remain calm."

Tom looked at Emilie, puzzled. He could see something blue sparkling in the light behind her. It looked like she had wings. He looked toward the waters in front of him and saw the mermaids and seahorses staring at him. He looked to the left and saw Nala and Cody standing to the side. He panicked and started to quickly backtrack on his hands and feet in the sand. He wanted to get as far away as possible from them. He was still weak and dazed, but he gathered all his strength to get up and run as fast as he could away from this bizarre, frightening scene. He thought, *Did I just see a dragon and a white tiger with wings? Were those giant seahorses?* He shook his head; he thought he must be having a bad dream and wanted to wake up immediately! He looked back again and saw everyone still staring at him. He screamed and ran with all the energy he had, determined to get as far away as possible or to wake up from this nightmare. He ran and ran and didn't look back.

Meanwhile, back at the shore, Emilie said, "Well, that went well!"

The mermaids and seahorses laughed.

Oriana said, "Good luck with the human! See you guys soon!"

The mermaids and seahorses took off toward the sea.

Nala said, "Shall we say thirty minutes before you go in?"

Emilie nodded and said, "Yes, then you and Cody will come thirty minutes after."

The three of them were used to the erratic behavior the visitors displayed. They had a plan for every circumstance, and their plans usually worked well. Thirty minutes would be enough time for Tom to run until he got tired. The beach went on for miles, and there was nothing but steep cliffs that surrounded it, which he wouldn't be able to climb. In the meantime, the three of them flew up to the cliffs where Archie and Georgina were standing and talked about last night's race.

After thirty minutes, Emilie was ready to find Tom. She said to Nala and Cody, "I'm off. Come in thirty minutes. That should give me enough time."

She flew from the cliff and spotted Tom by the rocks about one mile down. He was lying on the sand exhausted. Emilie flew down. He saw her coming and tried to climb the rocks to get away.

Emilie said to him, "Tom, please stop, I won't hurt you. I'm here to help you."

Tom looked back at her and gave up, as he didn't have the energy to run anymore, and his hands were bleeding and calloused. He said, "What do you want from me? Who are you, and what are you?"

Emilie said, "My name is Emilie, and I am a pixie from this land—Azar. What I want is for you to remain calm so we can speak and I can tell you what is happening."

Tom exclaimed, "Calm? Calm!? There was a dragon back there, and some sort of vicious, demonic-looking cat that looked like he wanted to eat me. Not to mention giant seahorses—and you! You have wings!? Am I dreaming? Is someone playing a bad joke on me? I want to go home! I have an important meeting I need to go to! I—I—I—"

"Enough!" Emilie shouted.

Tom was scared, as the pixie in front of him had turned a deep crimson color. He stopped talking and listened.

Emilie knew what she was doing, as she had used this trick many times. She would turn a terrifying red, and the visitor would fall silent and be ready to listen.

After Tom stopped rambling, Emilie turned back to her normal color and continued, "That is much better. Tom, I am going to tell you why you are here and what will happen during your stay here in Azar."

Tom listened intently.

Emilie continued, "One thing—this is not a dream, it is very real. You see, you've just stepped through a portal from your world that led to our world, which is in another dimension. Magical creatures like me and the others you saw on the beach live here. We all may look very scary, but we are harmless and only want to make sure you are safe for the nine days you are here."

Tom abruptly said, "Nine days? I can't stay here for nine days. I have a life back home. I have to go to work, and people will get worried!"

Emilie firmly said, "Look, you are here for nine days, but you will go back home only if you follow my directions."

Tom nodded and listened.

Emilie continued, "I am here because the Azarians have

entrusted me along with two other creatures to protect and care for you during the time you are here. We'll show you around our beautiful land and make sure you go back home safely when the portal opens."

Tom said, "What if I don't want to see your land? I can survive by myself and go back when the portal opens on my own."

Emilie said, "It wouldn't be possible for you to survive out here by yourself. You will perish, and I can't let that happen. Look, Tom, we can do this the hard way, or the easy way."

Tom gulped and said, "What is the hard way?"

Emilie said, "The hard way is, I bring you back to my home enclosed in a magic bubble, where you will be stuck for the nine-day period with no one to talk to."

Tom gulped and said, "And the easy way?"

Emilie said, "You willingly come with me and the other two hosts for the nine-day period. We will take care of you, show you the beautiful sights of Azar, and make sure you get home safely. What option would you like?"

Tom pondered the question. He thought he was a logical man, a successful businessman that made smart decisions every day. Wouldn't it be better to comply and go along with their plan? He wouldn't want to be stuck in this magic bubble for nine days. He would go crazy and wouldn't last. He definitely would not make it on his own in this land with fearsome creatures running about.

Tom said, "Fine, you have yourself a deal. I will do what you tell me. I just want to go home in one piece—please."

Emilie smiled, approached Tom with her hand outstretched, and said, "That's a deal!"

Tom shook Emilie's hand and looked at her closely, as her wings shimmered in the sunlight. He said, "You are a pixie. But you don't have a magic wand or pointy ears."

Emilie laughed. "No, I don't have those things. And one more very important thing—the other two that will be your caretakers are Nala, who was the white tiger, and Cody, the dragon, who you saw back there on the shore. They are harmless and will be here any minute to welcome you."

At that moment, Cody and Nala landed on the sand in front of them. They started walking toward Tom. Tom was frightened. Nala and Cody stopped when they saw panic in his eyes.

Emilie turned to Tom and said, "Calm down, Tom. They are your hosts and protectors and will not harm you. You must trust me, please!"

Tom looked at Nala and Cody, nodded, and said, "Okay."

Emilie waved Cody and Nala over.

Nala said, "Hello, Tom, I am Nala, and this is Cody. We won't harm you, so please don't be frightened."

Tom said nervously, "You can talk?"

"So can I!" Cody said.

Tom took a deep breath and looked at Emilie.

Emilie said, "All the creatures here on Azar can talk."

Tom nodded.

Emilie said, "Excuse us for one second."

The three of them went off to the side, and Emilie said, "Our plan worked. He is willing to go with us without a fight! Let's bring him home."

Nala and Cody were happy, as they didn't enjoy when the visitor was unpleasant or disagreeable.

Tom looked at these three creatures talking and wondered if he was in a dream or if he had simply gone mad. He was shocked that a tiger and dragon could talk, but considering the events of the day, this wasn't so bad.

Emilie turned around and said, "Now, Tom, we will go home to the Enchanted Forest. You will fly on Cody."

Tom laughed and said, "Enchanted Forest, like, in the fairytales? Wait—what? Did you say 'fly with Cody'? Fly on that dragon?"

Emilie said, "Yes, you will fly on Cody. It's very safe, and Nala and I will be there next to you."

Tom said, "Can't I just walk and follow you?"

Emilie said, "Look, Tom, this is how we will get around for the next nine days, so you'll need to get used to flying. I'll show you. It's very easy." Emilie jumped on Cody and said, "You sit like this and hold on tight. Cody, let's show."

They slowly lifted up, flew in a circle, and landed back on the beach.

Emilie said, "You see? Very easy. Come on, we must hurry home, as we have a lot to do."

Tom got up and slowly walked toward Cody. He took a deep breath and attempted to get on. He couldn't climb up because he was weak and had no energy.

Emilie said, "I'll help you." She climbed down, took Tom in her arms, placed Tom on Cody's back with ease, and climbed back up to sit in front.

Tom said, "Wow, you are a strong!"

Emilie said, "You ain't seen nothing yet! Now, hold on tight!"

Cody lifted up, and they flew away.

Tom held on tight and closed his eyes at first. Seconds later, he opened his eyes and looked to the right. Nala was flying alongside them. He looked down and saw lots of trees below and the beautiful colors of flower fields. He smiled, as he couldn't believe he was flying on a dragon next to a white tiger with wings. How bizarre this was! But he was pleasantly surprised and actually liked the view from up high. He thought that he had made the right decision to comply with their requests. The dream, so far—if it all was a dream—was going better than expected.

Emilie said, "How are you doing, Tom?"

Tom said, "Fine."

They continued on, and a forest came into view straight ahead. They were descending. Tom thought this must be the Enchanted Forest Emilie had spoken of.

Emilie said, "We're landing, hold on!"

They landed in an open field and walked along a trail that led into the forest. The trail was lined with a multitude of colorful flowers. Butterflies fluttered about with color markings that were unusual and rare. It was a lush tropical forest with many trees, brightly colored plants, and chirping birds. When Tom looked up, there was a brilliant rainbow peeking from behind the trees.

Emilie said, "We are almost there, just behind the rainbow."

Tom saw a large wooden house made up of big logs stacked upon each other. The house was decorated with vines and flowers hanging from the outer walls. There was a porch in front surrounded by pretty lights. There was a large garden fenced in with colorful flowers along the edges and a big, wide-open space of grass in the middle. Wooden chairs and a large picnic table were off to the side.

They arrived at the front steps, and Emilie turned to Tom and said, "Welcome, Tom. This is where you'll be staying for the next nine days." She turned to Cody and said, "Why don't you stay for a while? I'll get you something to eat and drink before you go home."

Cody nodded and went to the large space in the middle of the garden, where he lay down and rested.

Emilie said, "Come on in, Tom, I'll show you inside. You must be hungry and thirsty after today's journey." She waved him in, and Tom followed.

Nala said to Emilie, "I'll rest here for a bit." He lay down on the porch and fell asleep.

Tom entered a large room filled with a blue sofa, matching chairs, and a table in the middle. There were many paintings of what looked like animals dressed in human clothing on the walls. Tom looked at one with a peacock dressed in fine attire wearing a fancy hat. He stared at the painting for a few seconds and thought the peacock moved and winked at him.

"Did that peacock just wink at me?" he said to himself. He rubbed his eyes and looked at the picture again…nothing, no wink, no movement. He definitely thought he was seeing things, scratched his head, and continued on.

Emilie said, "This way, Tom, I have some food and drinks for you. Please sit down."

Tom walked into what seemed like a kitchen. There was a giant round table with four chairs with wide seats and odd backs that looked like tree branches sprouting green, fernlike leaves. There were no amenities like he had back home—no sink, no refrigerator, and no appliances. On a table in the corner was a blue vase with yellow daisies. The walls were painted a pretty pattern of swirls of blue, purple, and pink that was soothing to the eye. There was a big window on the far end looking out to the garden next to a door.

He looked out the window, and there was Cody sleeping soundly in the middle. The garden was surrounded by a plethora of colorful flowers. It reminded him of his home on the beach where he wished he could be right now.

He turned around, and surprisingly before him was a table set with utensils, plates, cups, a variety of pies, breads, and jellies, and a big pitcher of water. He wondered how all this had appeared, as it hadn't been here a second ago.

Emilie said, "Go on, Tom. You must be very hungry and thirsty. Here, sit down, and I'll pour you some water."

Tom sat and gulped down a large glass of water. He was starving and dug into a piece of pie. He was thrilled at how it tasted. He ate some bread with jam and was pleasantly surprised at the bursts of flavor everything had. He wasn't familiar with these types of berries, but they were delicious. He had another piece of pie and said, "What kind of pie is this?"

Emilie said, "That is dragonberry pie. Cody and his family baked that fresh today. Here, try some of this to drink." Emilie poured him a cup of Dragon's Delight.

Tom took a sip and liked it so much he finished the entire glass. "Wow, what is this?"

Emilie said, "It's Dragon's Delight. A mixture of dragonberries, dragonfruit, coconut, and other stuff. Here, try this one." She poured him a cup of dragon beer. "This is dragon beer."

Tom took a sip and said, "Ahhhhhh, this stuff is good. Just what I needed." He gulped down the rest and held out his cup for more.

Emilie said, "I think you may want to slow down on that one."

Tom said, "What do you mean? It's delicious!" He took another drink and started to yawn. He felt lightheaded and suddenly plopped his head on the table and fell asleep.

Emilie laughed and said, "You humans are real lightweights." Emilie shook her head. She said, "Well, off to bed you go, you'll need your rest for tomorrow to see the Council." She waved her hand above Tom's head, and he magically lifted up in the air. He was encompassed in a soft blue light that followed Emilie down a long, wide hallway and into the last room at the end of the hall.

The room was similar to Emilie's, as it had a wooden bed full of large, soft leaves. It also had a dresser, lamp, mirror, rocking chair, and table. It would suit Tom's needs for his short period of time on Azar.

Emilie laid Tom on the soft bed of leaves and placed a blanket over him. She left the room, and Tom slept soundly through the night.

DAY 2
THE COUNCIL

Tom woke the next day in his bed rested and full of energy. He looked around and wondered how he had gotten to this bed. He felt the soft leaves cushioning him and couldn't remember when he had slept so well. He looked at his surroundings and was disappointed that he was still in this dream, though he was beginning to think that it was all very real. His hands hurt, as they had cuts and were calloused. His clothes were torn and ragged.

He got out of bed, went to the dresser and mirror, looked at himself, and cringed at how horrible he looked. He wondered if there was a shower or bath, as he really needed one.

Emilie walked in the room and said, "Good morning, Tom.

How did you sleep?"

Tom said, "Good, I slept very well. I guess you were right, that drink you gave me knocked me out."

Emilie said, "Yes, the dragon beer did it to you. But we must get going, as you are going to meet the Council today."

Tom said, "What is the Council?"

Emilie said, "The Council is made up of three of the wisest creatures on Azar. They want to ask you some questions and get to know you. It's very easy. Just be honest and answer their questions, and you can ask them questions as well."

Tom said, "Okay, I guess that would be easy enough. Do you think I can borrow some clothes as mine are not looking so good?"

Emilie said, "I've taken care of that and called the best seamstress on Azar. She'll be here shortly! In the meantime, why don't you wash up?" She pointed at the towels, hair brush, toothbrush, and toothpaste that sat on the dresser next to a bowl of water.

Tom said, "How did you do that? That wasn't there a minute

ago. Never mind. I guess I have to get used to this stuff-appearing-and-disappearing act."

Emilie said, "Now, if you would like to wash off all that dirtiness, especially the black goo stuck in your hair, there is a stream and waterfall out back through that door and past the garden. Let's get going because Jane Peacock will be here shortly!" Emilie walked out the door.

Tom touched the top of his head and could feel something gooey and gross knotted in his hair. He needed a bath ASAP! He took a towel and walked out the back door through the garden. He continued down a stony path and heard the waterfall. He reached the end of the path and was amazed by what was in front of him. Bright turquoise waters gleamed in the sunlight, and a tall, majestic waterfall stood in the middle of them. It was absolutely stunning.

He took off his ragged clothes and placed his foot in the water to feel the temperature…it was perfect. He dipped into the water and scrubbed the soot and grime off his hair and skin as best he could. He heard some rustling in the bushes, quickly turned around, and saw Nala at the edge of the waters smiling down at him.

Nala said, "Emilie said to hurry because the seamstress will be here very soon."

Tom nodded. Nala went back to the house. He thought he really needed to get used to this enormous white tiger, as he'd be living with him for the next nine days. He still couldn't believe that Nala and Cody even spoke, but he knew there were bigger surprises ahead of him that would be more shocking than this. He got out of the water, dried himself off, and went inside to prepare for the seamstress.

Tom quickly got dressed in the same torn and dirty clothes. Emilie called Tom to the parlor. Tom walked in and saw Emilie standing next to the door. At the other side of the room was a peacock wearing a fine tailored dress with a fancy purple hat. She wore tiny spectacles and looked like the subject of the painting he had seen on the wall. In fact, she was standing right next to it, and it looked just like her.

Emilie said, "Tom, I would like you to meet Jane Peacock, Azar's best seamstress."

Jane Peacock took a bow and said, "Why, pleased to meet you, Tom. And, yes, I am the one in the picture right here." She pointed to the picture on the wall.

Tom said, "Nice to meet you, Jane Peacock."

Jane Peacock was very tall and broad, and her feathers were beautiful. Her tail fanned out in feathers of blue, green and purple, which gleamed in the light and matched her outfit perfectly. Tom admitted that this peacock was the best-dressed peacock he had ever seen.

Next to Jane Peacock was a small hedgehog carrying a notepad and a case that held threads, a pin cushion, and measuring tapes.

Jane Peacock said, "This is my assistant, Harry the Hedgehog. He will be getting your measurements and assisting me in making your fine clothes."

Harry the Hedgehog bowed but didn't say a thing. Tom bowed back to Harry. Harry was also dressed very nicely. He was wearing a smart gray coat jacket and a red bowtie.

Jane Peacock said, "Now, let's see what we have to work with here." Jane Peacock circled Tom, looking at him up and down, and said, "Well, you have very broad shoulders and are tall for a human. My clothes will fit you well. Harry, please get the measurements so we can get started."

Harry said, "Yes, ma'am!" He got his measuring tape and wrapped it around his neck then got his notepad and started to float in the air toward Tom.

Tom yelped and stepped back.

Emilie said, "It's okay, Tom, he needs to take your measurements. Please, you must get used to creatures flying and floating in the air, okay?"

Tom nodded and stayed still as Harry took his measurements. Harry first took his neck, bust, waist, and hip length. Then he asked Tom to straighten his arms out, and he continued to take the rest of his measurements, including those of his feet.

When Harry was done, Jane Peacock looked at the scribbles on the notepad. She turned to Emilie and said, "Okay, I've got the measurements. I know you are meeting the Council this afternoon, so I'll be back in a jiff with Tom's clothes!" Jane Peacock and Harry quickly walked out the door.

In the meantime, Emilie took Tom to the kitchen where they had a breakfast of flapjacks, berry juice, and fresh fruit. Nala was already at the table eating, and Tom said, "This looks good. I'm starving." He sat down and dug into the stack of flapjacks.

They finished breakfast and went out to the garden where Nala lay down and started scratching his back on the grass by wiggling back and forth. Tom smiled at Nala, as he looked like his neighbor's dog scratching his back on the rug, but maybe twenty times bigger.

He took a seat and looked at the garden in front of him. He then looked up and saw a huge dragon soaring way up in the sky with fire coming from his mouth.

Emilie said, "Cody is here. Make sure you don't stand in the middle of the garden."

Tom was thankful that the fire-breathing creature was Cody and not some other unfriendly beast. In fact, he laughed at the thought that a dragon was just about to land a few feet in front of him.

Cody circled the house and did a few tricks in the air. He twirled and made zig-zag motions.

Emilie said, "He just likes to show off. Cody is actually Azar's Race to the Moon winner. He is the fastest creature on Azar!"

Tom said, "I can believe that. He seems to be having lots of fun up there."

After a short acrobatic show, Cody landed in Emilie's garden. Cody said, "Hi, Emilie, Nala. Hi, Tom, how ya doing today?"

Tom said, "Good. Just ate some excellent flapjacks."

Suddenly, a squawking sound came from above. Jane Peacock and Harry the Hedgehog were coming in to land. Jane Peacock was carrying a big bag from her mouth like a stork carrying a baby. They landed in front of Cody and the others.

Jane Peacock said, "Well, hello there, Cody! You did so well at the Moon Races! Congratulations again! Tom, here are your clothes. Let's try them on and see if they fit you."

Emilie said, "That was really fast, Jane."

Jane Peacock said, "Well, I know the urgency. I mean, look at what he is wearing, it's just awful, and he needs to look his best in front of the Council this afternoon."

Emilie, Jane, and Harry went in the house and sat in the parlor while Tom tried on the clothes. After a few minutes, Tom came out to the parlor smiling. Tom said, "These clothes fit perfectly, and this material is so soft. The shoes fit great. Thank you!"

Jane Peacock said, "Look at you, it does fit pretty well. I've made enough clothes for you to last till you go back home. If you need anything else, just let me know! I'll see y'all at the Council meeting!" Jane Peacock and Harry walked out the door and flew off.

Emilie turned to Tom and said, "The clothes look very good, Tom. Now you are ready to face the Council."

Emilie and Tom went outside to the garden and sat down. Tom asked, "The Council meeting sounds very important. What will they ask me?"

Emilie said, "You don't have to be worried about the Council. It's just a formality that all visitors must go through. The Council consists of three of the wisest creatures on Azar. They are Theodore the Great Owl, Jane Peacock, whom you have already met, and lastly, Bakari the Emperor Cat. You will stand in front of them, and they'll ask you questions. You can ask them questions as well. It's very simple, and it won't take long. They want to make sure that you are not a danger to Azar. I know you will be just fine, Tom."

Tom said, "Sounds intimidating to me."

Emilie said, "Come on, we should go. We don't want to be late. Cody will take us there." They all flew off to meet the Council.

They landed at Pamplemousse Peak atop a large mountain surrounded by orchards of trees filled with big pink and yellow fruit.

Emilie said, "This fruit is called pamplemousse; hence, Pamplemousse Peak. It's very sweet and tasty. It's mixed with other fruits on Azar to make a delicious drink called pamplemousse punch."

Nala said, "Mmm-mmm, pamplemousse punch is one of my favorites." Nala licked his lips.

They walked on a path that led to an area with rocks and boulders. Tom heard water rushing in the distance. Cody said, "I'll wait out here and stand guard."

"So you can take a nap?" Nala said, laughing.

Cody said, "Well, now that you mentioned it, I will take a nap."

Emilie, Nala, and Tom continued up the stony path that turned into a tropical rainforest with cascading waterfalls on each side. Healthy green foliage with colorful flowers and plants grew everywhere. Tom was amazed at the beauty of this place.

He looked in the waters and saw a very large, fish-like creature popping its head out. It said hello. More of the creatures swam by and said hello to Tom.

Tom said, "Are those dolphins? Blue dolphins?"

Emilie said, "Yes, this is Dolphin Lagoon, and they are the blue dolphins from Meridien. They will bear witness at the Council. We are almost there. Be careful not to fall because the rocks are slippery."

Tom nodded and smiled at the playful dolphins following him down the path.

They finally came to a large, open lagoon with huge waterfalls cascading down each side. The dolphins made loud squeaking noises announcing to the Council that the visitor was here. Right above the lagoon was a large platform structure that was part of the mountain. This was where the Council sat.

Emilie said to Tom, "Stand there in the middle, and they will come."

Tom was very nervous at this point. There was a squawk from the sky, and they looked up. A large bird hovered above and landed in the middle of the rock structure perched in front of them. It was Theodore the Owl.

Theodore wore a tailored dark green coat vest with gold trim. He wore gold-rimmed spectacles. He looked down at the blue dolphins and acknowledged their presence. He looked at Tom for a moment then turned to Emilie and Nala and nodded at them.

There was another squawk from above, and Tom immediately recognized Jane Peacock as she slowly descended and landed to the right of Theodore. Jane Peacock was impeccably dressed in a purple-and-gold dress. She wore a matching hat made of peacock feathers embellished with blue and purple jewels. She said hello to Theodore and nodded to Emilie and Nala. She then looked at Tom and smiled.

Then came a loud and deep growl that sent chills down Tom's spine. He was frightened and turned to Emilie, wide-eyed with fear. She gave him a reassuring look. Tom saw a large black cat slowly creeping out from behind the waterfall. He thought this must be

Bakari the Emperor Cat.

Bakari stood tall and handsome. He looked fierce. He had a long, thick, and dense mane around his neck that made him look very regal. His coat was entirely black and shined in the light. He had a long tail with a tuft of longer fur at the end. He had elegant wings that reminded Tom of the mythical creatures he used to read about when he was a kid. He stood at the bottom of the mountain and looked up to where Theodore and Jane Peacock were seated before he looked Tom straight in the eye. He then swiftly and stealthily climbed the mountain. He reached the platform, sat on the left side of Theodore, and gave a big roar.

All three of them faced Tom.

Theodore spoke first. "Welcome, Tom, to the Council of Azar. I am Theodore, and to my right is Jane Peacock, and to my left is Bakari. We also have the blue dolphins here to bear witness and to represent the Kingdom of Meridien."

The dolphins squeaked and nodded their heads as they looked up at the Council.

"Now, I'm sure you are wondering why you are standing in

front of us today, and it is because we Azarians would like to welcome you to our magical land and at the same time want to make sure your stay will be most enjoyable for you and for us. This is also a chance for us to get to know you and for you to ask us any questions you may have. We will go first."

Jane Peacock cleared her throat and said, "Tom, where are you from on Earth?"

Tom said, "I am from California. It's located in the United States of America."

Theodore said, "And what is your profession? What do you do?"

Tom said, "I am a lawyer. My specialty is international corporate law."

Theodore said, "Ah, a lawyer. Intelligent and well-traveled, I presume."

Bakari, in a deep and powerful voice, said, "What are your intentions here on Azar?"

Tom said, "I don't have any intentions here, sir. I mean, I have told my hosts that I will do what is asked of me. I would just like to go home as soon as possible…in one piece, that is."

Bakari laughed and roared. He said, "One piece? Well, of course, one piece! Why would you think otherwise?" Bakari had a big smile that showed off his huge, pearly-white fangs, which gleamed in the light. Tom gulped at the size of his fangs.

Jane Peacock said, "Bakari, will you stop that? You are frightening the poor human with that smirk on your face!"

Bakari quickly shut his mouth, turned to Theodore, and nodded his head for him to continue.

Theodore said, "Now that we know a little more about you, Tom, we must set some rules for you that all visitors must follow. These are called the Three Golden Rules. We have these very important rules because, in the past, visitors have had some strange habits that we did not appreciate and definitely will not tolerate. These rules must be obeyed at all times during your stay."

Theodore waved his wand, and a giant scroll floated toward Tom. The scroll unraveled and read on the top in big gold letters, "The Three Golden Rules."

Theodore continued, "Please read aloud the first rule, Tom."

Tom took a deep breath and in a nervous voice read the first Golden Rule,

"GOLDEN RULE #1
Do not harm or eat the creatures."

Theodore said, "That is self-explanatory—do not harm or eat the creatures of Azar or the sea creatures of Meridien. Do you have any questions about that rule, Tom?"

"No, I understand that rule perfectly clear, but, um, well, I would like to say that I would never eat any creatures on Azar or Meridien, but also the creatures can't eat me, right?" Tom said nervously. "I mean, there are very big creatures roaming around here, and I would think that rule would apply to me as well?"

Theodore, Jane Peacock, and Bakari started to laugh. The blue dolphins laughed as well. Nala and Emilie looked at each other trying not to laugh aloud, too.

Theodore said, "No, Tom, we will not eat you. We do not eat

humans nor do we harm humans. We are happy with the delicacies here on Azar. Your guides and protectors will not let any harm come to you during your stay. All visitors we had in the past have made it back to their world safely…well, now, I take it back, one did not, but that was because he violated the rules, which I am sure you will not."

Bakari exclaimed, "Yes! It was the human hunter, and we took care of him!" Bakari growled and snarled.

Theodore continued, "You have nothing to worry about, Tom, you will be fine as long as you follow the rules. Now, continue onto Golden Rule number two. Please read that."

Tom said,

"GOLDEN RULE #2
No littering allowed."

Theodore said, "In the past, we have had problems with visitors not cleaning up after themselves. It was a pesky habit of leaving trash or unwanted items wherever and whenever they like, even in our beautiful waters. We ask that you respect our environment and clean after yourselves and put things back in its proper place as it should be. Do you have any questions about this rule, Tom?"

Tom said, "No, I understand that rule completely. You don't have to worry about me because I am a very tidy person."

Theodore said, "Very good, now please read the last Golden Rule."

Tom said,

"GOLDEN RULE #3
Destruction of vegetation and sea habitat is strictly prohibited."

Theodore said, "Now, Tom, this is a very important rule. We Azarians and the creatures of Meridien love where we live. We love every leaf, flower, rock, tree, marine plant, and marine flower in our habitats. It is what makes our world beautiful. We would like to keep it this way, and we ask that our visitors respect that. Do you understand this rule, Tom?"

Tom said, "Yes, I do understand."

Theodore said, "Very good. Now please read on to the paragraph below."

Tom continued, "Violation of the above Three Golden Rules will result in severe punishment and may include death." Tom gulped. "Death?"

Theodore said, "Why, of course! You see, we have established the Three Golden Rules as a result of our past visitors' behavior. We would like to have our lands the way it was prior to your arrival. Don't worry, Tom, it really never resorted to death…. Well, there was one case that almost—but we won't get into that."

Bakari snarled and growled.

"Anyhow, I believe you won't have to worry about that. I think you will be just fine. Now, if you agree to the Golden Rules set forth to you today, please sign your name on the bottom line, and we can go on about our business."

Tom looked for something to write with. Theodore said, "Here, use this."

Theodore threw a stick in the air, and it floated toward Tom. It turned into a white feathered fountain pen, wiggled around, and said to Tom, "Go on, I won't bite! I'm just a pen."

Tom, in disbelief, grabbed the pen and signed his name at the bottom of the scroll.

The dolphins did acrobatic stunts, jumps, and backward slides on the water. Jane Peacock flapped her wings in joy. Nala and Emilie were relieved now that the formalities had passed. Theodore and Jane Peacock flew down to welcome Tom to Azar.

Bakari jumped from the rock and landed right in front of Tom. Tom, frightened, took a few steps back, as Bakari was even scarier and intimidating up close. Everyone was silent as Bakari, who was giant standing next to Tom, walked up very slowly and started to sniff Tom up and down. Tom stood still and tried to remain calm.

Bakari stepped back and said, "You will come visit me at my home on Pinnacle Mountain, and we will have a little chat." Bakari smiled, showing his huge white fangs.

Tom nervously said, "Of…of…of course, Mr. Bakari, I mean, Emperor Bakari."

Bakari turned around, spread his magnificent wings, and flew off into the moonlit sky.

Theodore said, "Well, Tom, I will see you again soon. Emilie, Nala, and Cody will take good care of you and show you around our beautiful lands. Don't forget the Golden Rules, and maybe one day those rules will come in handy in your world." Theodore winked and flew away.

Jane Peacock said, "You must come to my house for some tea and cookies, and I will show you around my fabulous gardens!"

Tom said, "Yes, thank you, thank you very much!"

Jane Peacock flew away. The blue dolphins said farewell and disappeared in the waters.

Emilie said, "Well, Tom, you survived the Council, and now it's time to have some fun!" They all took off on Cody and flew back to the Enchanted Forest.

DAY 3
THE UNICORNS

IT WAS MORNING, AND TOM AWOKE BRIGHT AND EARLY. He got up, got ready, and headed to the kitchen, wondering where everyone was. He looked out the window and saw Emilie and Nala motioning him to come outside. He stepped out back, and breakfast was ready on the table.

Emilie said, "Let's eat! Cody already ate. He was starving and couldn't wait."

They sat down and ate while Cody laid on the grass scratching his back, wiggling back and forth.

Tom laughed at Cody and said, "What are we doing today?"

Emilie said, "Well, I was thinking we go and visit the unicorns."

Tom said in surprise, "Unicorns? They are real? Sounds good to me!"

They quickly finished breakfast and headed out on foot.

Emilie said, "We'll walk along the path through the forest and should be there in an hour."

Tom said, "We're not flying?"

Emilie said, "No. It's not that far out. Besides, it's good exercise for us all."

They walked through the Enchanted Forest, and Tom smelled a flowery scent in the air that reminded him of his mom. He hadn't seen his mom or family back home for two years because of his busy schedule at work. He missed his mom and told himself he would definitely visit them in New York this year for the holidays.

They walked farther, and the scent got stronger. Tom said, "What is that smell? It smells like roses."

Nala said, "Your nose is correct. Look ahead."

He could only see a bunch of trees in front of them. They walked farther and found themselves surrounded by a large number of tall trees with thick trunks. Each tree had a multitude of pink flowers blooming from its branches. Tom looked closer and couldn't believe his eyes. He said, "Are those roses? Roses grow on trees here?"

Emilie said, "Of course, they do. They grow everywhere."

Tom said, "Amazing! They grow on shrubs where I'm from. My mom would go crazy if she saw these trees. It's her favorite flower and the smell of her favorite perfume."

Suddenly the rose tree that Tom stood near yawned out loud. A friendly face materialized on the tree trunk and smiled. Tom was startled and jumped back and hid behind Cody with fright.

The rose tree said, "Well, hello, fellow Azarians! And who is this creature here?"

Emilie said, "Hello, Mr. Rose! Did we wake you? I'm sorry if we did. This is Tom, the visitor."

Mr. Rose said, "Ahhh, yes, I've heard about you, Tom, through the grapevine." Mr. Rose winked at him.

Tom didn't say a word, as he was still shocked.

Emilie said, "Tom, it's okay. The rose trees talk, too. They won't harm you. Come out here and say hello to Mr. Rose."

Tom stepped forward and said, "I'm sorry. I've never heard a tree talk before."

Mr. Rose laughed and said, "Of course. We wouldn't harm you, Tom, right, guys? Say hello to Tom."

All of a sudden, faces appeared on all the tree trunks. The trees said, "Hello, Tom!" "Welcome, Tom!" The loud sound of the trees speaking at once freaked him out, and Tom covered his ears.

Mr. Rose said, "Okay, guys, let's quiet down now." All the trees became silent, and Mr. Rose turned to Tom and said, "So, Tom, I heard that roses are your mom's favorite flower, did you say?"

Tom said, "Well, yes, she loves roses, especially red roses, they are her favorite."

Mr. Rose said, "That is very nice to hear. We can be red, too, you know. Watch this!"

All the flowers on the trees slowly turned from pink to a beautiful, vibrant red. Everyone looked up, and Tom had a huge smile on his face.

Mr. Rose said, "You see, Tom, I knew we could make you smile. In fact, we can change to any color we want." Mr. Rose shouted to all the rose trees, "Rose Trees of Azar, let us dazzle Tom!"

Each tree slowly turned their roses from bright red to a mixture of different shades of color. There were yellow, purple, pink, peach, lilac, white, dark red, orange, and blue roses everywhere! It really was a spectacular sight to see! Tom was amazed at how each flower had magically transformed right before his eyes. He closed his eyes and took a deep breath of the alluring scent surrounding him. He opened his eyes and turned to all the rose trees of Azar and sincerely said, "Thank you. This is absolutely spectacular!"

Mr. Rose said, "It was our pleasure, Tom. Come back and visit us real soon, you hear!"

They all said their goodbyes and continued down the path.

They walked out of the forest and came to a lake where they stopped to rest. Cody and Nala lay down near the rocks. Tom splashed his face with water and sat near Nala. He felt safe around Nala and Cody now, as he knew they were there to protect him and would cause him no harm. Tom also knew now that this was not a dream; it was all very real.

He sighed and looked up at the sky that was blue and clear. He took a breath of fresh air and realized how clean and crisp the air was. He noticed he hadn't had any asthma symptoms since he'd arrived here. He was very happy about that, as he had to use an inhaler often at home. He thought, *It isn't so bad being in Azar, it could be a lot worse.* He laughed at the idea.

Emilie said to Tom, "What's so funny?"

Tom said, "Nothing, I was just admiring the blue skies and the clean, fresh air you have here in Azar. It's not like this back home."

Emilie said, "What do you mean?"

Tom said, "Where I live, the sky is not clear and blue like this. In fact, it's a hazy brownish color sometimes."

Emilie said, "Brown? Why is it brown?"

Tom said, "The pollutants, or smog, turns it brown. There are other cities around the world where it's worse than where I live. In fact, in other countries, their skies are black because of the pollution in the air. You Azarians are very lucky."

Emilie said, "That is terrible—brown and black skies! Don't you care about your environment or health? Is it not a big concern on Earth?"

Tom sighed and said, "Of course, I care about my health and my environment but…but…it's a long story, and I don't want to bore you with the details. You wouldn't understand."

He looked at Emilie as she waited for an answer. Tom contemplated how he was going to explain this complicated matter to a pixie in simple terms. He thought for a minute, then took a deep breath and said, "You see, humans cannot fly like the creatures of Azar. We don't have wings or magic wands that can make us disappear and reappear somewhere else. We depend on things like cars and trucks to go places and big factories to produce things that we need in our daily lives. Now, these things need fossil fuels to run, such as coal and gasoline, which create pollution in the air, which turns the skies a brownish or black color. It's a big global problem that a lot of people are concerned about."

Emilie said, "That is very sad. Can't you do something about this? Azarians would not tolerate something that would harm our environment or the creatures. We care about Azar and would stop the problem immediately!"

Tom said, "I wish there was something that could be done, but it is a very big problem that we can't take care of just like that. It's complicated and involves many factors. Believe me, if I had my way, there would be far less pollution in the air. But I am only one person in a world that has eight billion people. Unfortunately, I'm not able to make a difference."

Emilie got up and said, "I disagree with that, Tom. I believe you can make a difference."

Tom was puzzled.

Emilie continued, "Enough of this gloomy talk. Let's go visit the unicorns, they are waiting!"

They continued through grass fields and up a mountain slope. Emilie said, "We are almost there." At the top of the mountain were rows of trees with purple, star-shaped fruit dangling from the branches.

As they got closer, Tom said, "What kind of trees are these? Are these fruits hanging from them? They are shaped like stars."

Emilie said, "Yes, these are starfruits. The unicorns love these. They're very tasty, try one." Emilie took one off the tree and started eating. Nala and Cody did the same.

Tom followed suit. He took a bite out of one and said, "It's a fig. A starfig fruit. These are way cooler looking than the ones we have back home. They taste delicious." Tom looked closely at one of the branches and asked, "What is this iridescent purple dust on some of the branches?" He looked closer. "There are little stars in the dust, and it's glowing. It's all over the ground here, too."

Emilie said, "Oh, that's just unicorn dust. It's what the unicorns leave behind. A unicorn was there where you are standing eating the starfruit."

Tom heard a rustle of leaves in the distance. He looked around hoping to see a unicorn, but there was nothing. He walked away from the group, as they were busy eating.

Nala said, "Don't wander too far."

Tom nodded. He saw something in the corner of his eye about fifty feet away. He crept closer to take a look. He heard more leaves rustling and turned around, and there in front of him stood a beautiful white unicorn.

The unicorn had a long mane that was braided and intertwined with little flowers. He had a long and thick flowing tail that gleamed in the light. His horn was pearly white and twirled from the base to the tip. His wings, resting at his sides, were large and elegant.

The unicorn saw Tom and started to approach him. He stopped a few feet away and looked straight into Tom's eyes. Tom thought the unicorn was saying something, but he didn't speak, so Tom dismissed the idea. He got closer and slowly reached out and patted the unicorn on the head, stroking gently the creature's white, shiny hair.

The unicorn neighed in contentment. Tom smiled and rubbed the unicorn's neck. He remembered summers he spent on his aunt's farm helping harvest the crops and caring for the animals. He loved the horses most of all. He really missed those carefree days.

Emilie, Cody, and Nala appeared. The unicorn turned to them and bowed regally.

Emilie walked toward them and said, "I see you have met Bijoux." Emilie patted Bijoux on the head and said, "How you doing, boy?" She gave Bijoux a big hug and said, "Bijoux, this is Tom. He is the visitor from Earth."

Bijoux nodded then turned around and motioned with his head for them to follow.

Tom said, "They don't speak?"

Emilie said, "The unicorns don't speak out loud. They speak through their minds. They understand what we're saying, but they communicate mentally without speaking. I believe you humans call it 'mental telepathy.' You wouldn't be able to hear what the unicorns are saying, only Azarians are able to." Emilie paused and added, "But there was one visitor that could speak with them. He wasn't human. He was from another planet in your galaxy, a planet that was barren and lifeless. He spoke to his people by mental telepathy, so communicating with the unicorns was easy for him. In fact, the unicorns really liked him, as all the creatures of Azar did. He was very quiet, courteous, and always wanted to learn about new things and how we did things here. He and actually two others were the only visitors that could communicate with the unicorns."

Tom was very curious to know who these visitors were that could speak with the unicorns.

Emilie walked with Bijoux up front. The rest followed them along the path. Tom turned to Nala and Cody and said, "Do you guys know what visitors Emilie was referring to? Was it aliens? You know, scary creatures with big black eyes, long skinny fingers, and legs? Also, their heads are kinda weirdly shaped…bigger on top with a narrow face. You know, real scary-looking?"

Cody and Nala looked at each other, puzzled. Cody said, "No. I don't remember any visitors looking scary."

Nala interrupted, exclaiming, "There was one! That human hunter was scary-looking. He had craziness in his eyes. And we know what happened to him!"

Cody said, "Oh yeah, now, he was scary! But you should ask Theodore. He would be able to answer your question."

Tom was very curious and made a mental note to ask Theodore

about these mysterious visitors who could talk with the unicorns.

They continued through the orchard and heard a rumbling in the distance. Tom knew right away it was the unicorns running—many unicorns, judging by the volume of the rumbling.

They reached the edge of the orchard and walked into an open field where the unicorns were running in a giant circle. Bijoux stepped forward, turned to Emilie, and said something without speaking. He then joined a group of three unicorns standing on the side talking amongst each other. Bijoux spoke with them, and they all turned and looked at Tom. It seemed the unicorn in the middle was the leader. He was larger in size and muscular, and there was an air of superiority about him. He had more flowers in his mane, and his horn was the color of gold and shined brilliantly in the sunlight.

Bijoux and the unicorn with the gold horn walked toward them.

Emilie said, "Hello, Willow. I've brought the visitor. His name is Tom, and he would like to spend some time with you and the others."

Tom remained calm and cool on the outside, but inside he was very excited. He thought the pictures in the storybooks that he read to his five-year-old niece didn't do them justice, as they were even more beautiful and magical up close. He would love to ride one, but he thought that might be asking too much.

Emilie turned to Tom and said, "Tom, this is Willow, and he is the leader of the unicorns. Willow told me you are a person of nature. A human who loves horses? Is that true, Tom?"

Tom was surprised at Emilie's words. He wondered if Willow had just read his mind, or perhaps Bijoux had read his mind back at the starfruit trees?

Tom said, "Well, yes, I spent a lot of time with horses on my aunt's farm when I was young, and I love horses, yes, I do."

Emilie smiled. "Good. Willow will take you around the land of the unicorns, and I'll go with you. Nala and Cody will stay here and do what they do best…take a nap."

Everyone laughed. Cody and Nala rested in the shade.

Emilie said to Tom, "Tom, you will ride Willow, and I will go with Bijoux."

Tom said, "Wait, you mean, ride on a unicorn?"

Emilie said, "Of course! Willow said you wanted to ride on a unicorn. You do know how to ride, right?"

Tom thought to himself, *They can read my mind! How crazy is this?*

He said, "Yes, but I've ridden on horses, not on unicorns, and Willow is much bigger than what I'm used to."

Emilie said, "It's the same thing. Willow will make sure you are safe. Now get on, and let's go!"

Tom attempted to get on, but Willow was just too tall. He needed help.

Nala came over and said, "Step on me, Tom."

He stepped on Nala's back and got on Willow with ease. He had never ridden bareback before but thought it should be fine. He moved forward to get a better grip.

Emilie said, "You can hold onto Willow's mane, he doesn't mind."

Tom nodded and took a hold of the mane. Willow and Bijoux started to walk then sped up into a trot. As they trotted, Tom studied Willow's physique. His coat was very healthy and shiny, and his hair was lush and thick. He looked at the structure of Willow's golden horn. It twirled from the bottom to the top and was very thick near the base and sharpened toward the tip. It looked solid gold because of its beautiful, lustrous sheen. Willow, as well as all the other unicorns, was all muscle and strength. They had fantastic physiques, which suggested superior strength to their counterparts on Earth.

They went faster into a gallop and approached the large circle of running unicorns. Tom held on tightly, as they were quickly picking up speed. They were headed straight for the circle, and the unicorns made an opening in which for them to enter. Willow ran fast, and Tom held on with excitement. He looked to the side, and there was Emilie and Bijoux right next to him. Emilie smiled, enjoying the ride just as much as he was. They went faster and faster and circled around a dozen times then broke off and headed toward the other side of the field near the mountain rocks.

Tom was thrilled. "That was amazing! I've never gone that fast before."

Emilie said, "It was great, wasn't it? You know, they can go faster than that. Perhaps if you are up to it, we can have a little race later." Emilie winked.

Tom said, "I'm definitely up for that!"

Willow spoke to Emilie. Emilie turned to Tom and said, "We will go to Unicorn Falls."

They headed up a path that led to a lush green area filled with colorful, tropical flowers and big, leafy plants. They walked along the path and saw birds with large, brightly colored beaks that looked similar to toucans but were much larger than the ones back home. They walked farther and heard waterfalls. After a few minutes, the path ended, and they finally arrived at Unicorn Falls.

It was a breathtaking sight. The area was of considerable size with about a dozen waterfalls cascading into several pools. Unicorns were everywhere—resting along the rocks, drinking, and taking a swim in the waters. A few blue dolphins from Meridien were also here enjoying the falls. There was unicorn dust everywhere. Unicorns came up to get a glimpse of the visitor, and Tom smiled and said hello to all of them. Tom thought about his niece and how she would have loved to see this. It was truly magical.

Emilie was having a great time swimming amongst the unicorns and blue dolphins. She shouted to Tom, "Why don't you come in for a swim? The water feels great!"

Tom took off his shoes and shirt and jumped right in. They swam and played with the dolphins for a while. Then Willow walked over to Emilie and said something. It was time to go.

Emilie motioned Tom over. Tom said farewell to all of the unicorns and dolphins. They followed Willow and Bijoux out of the falls, continued on in a new direction, and ended up in a field filled with rows and rows of huge yellow sunflowers.

Emilie said to Tom, "Shall we race?"

Tom smiled and said, "Bring it on!"

Emilie waved her hand, and Tom rose in the air and plopped straight on Willow's back. Emilie was positioned on Bijoux, leaning forward and low over Bijoux's back. Tom got in the same position and held on very tightly.

Willow said to Tom, "Are you ready? Just hold on tight, and you'll be fine."

Tom nodded and thought, *Did Willow just speak to me?* He was surprised but at the same time needed to concentrate, or this could go very badly.

They were off. Willow and Bijoux jolted and propelled forward with incredible speed. How they had been running earlier was nothing compared to this. Emilie and Bijoux were ahead by a length. Tom was ecstatic, as he had never gone as fast as this. He suddenly felt a lift, looked down, and saw they were a foot off the ground. They were flying in the air!

Tom looked at Emilie. She and Bijoux were up in the air as well.

Tom said, "Woo-hoo! We're flying!" He looked back and saw massive white wings flapping behind him. He looked at Emilie, and she pointed below. Tom looked down and saw the lake and terrain they'd crossed and the grass field where the unicorns were gathered. He could see Cody and Nala resting by the trees.

They started to descend and landed. Tom got off and looked at Willow, as he knew this was the end of the tour. He affectionately patted Willow on his neck and head and said, "Thank you, Willow."

Willow said, "You're welcome, Tom. It was our pleasure.

And tell your niece that unicorns do exist."

Tom was thrilled that he could actually hear the unicorns speak. He said goodbye to Bijoux, and they all flew home to the Enchanted Forest.

DAY 4
JANE PEACOCK

TOM WOKE UP BRIGHT AND EARLY. AFTER HIS encounters with the unicorns, he was in great spirits and looking forward to today's adventure. He wondered what they were going to do today. He jumped out of bed and got ready for the day. Breakfast was ready as usual. Tom liked the foods of Azar, but he was starting to miss the meals back home. He was more of a steak-and-potatoes kind of guy, but being that Azarians were vegetarians, he would have to wait until he got back home. He ate and drank his pamplemousse punch, his drink of choice for breakfast because of the energy it gave him. This and the Dragon's Delight were his favorite.

He finished breakfast and wondered where everyone was. He

got up and looked through the window and saw them outside. They were lined up doing weird dance moves in slow motion that looked very familiar. He went outside and didn't say a word, as they were in deep concentration. Tom knew what these movements were called but couldn't quite put his finger on it. He thought hard for a moment and suddenly remembered.

"Tai Chi!" he exclaimed.

All three of them stopped and looked at him. Tom was embarrassed for blurting his thought out loud. He apologized and sat quietly on the bench. They all continued to do the flowing movements of Tai Chi.

Emilie said, "Good morning, Tom. Did you have a good night's sleep?"

Tom said, "Yes, I did. Where did you learn Thai Chi?"

Emilie said, "We learned Tai Chi from a visitor from China. He was doing this every morning and taught us how to do it. I find it very relaxing."

Cody and Nala at the same time said, "Very relaxing."

Everyone continued the movements in sync.

Nala said, in a calm and soothing voice, "You see, Tom, Tai Chi is an art embracing the mind, body, and spirit. The essential principles are to have your mind and body as one while controlling your movements and breathing. This creates inner energy and serenity."

Cody added, also in a calm and soothing voice, "The ultimate purpose of this is to cultivate the life energy within us to flow *smoothly* and *powerfully*, thus, creating harmony."

They ended the session by reaching their arms up in a circular motion, bringing their arms down with their hands in the prayer position, and breathing out. They then bowed.

Tom clapped and said, "That was awesome! You said you learned this from a visitor?"

Emilie said, "Yes, he also taught us the ancient Chinese martial art of Kung Fu." Emilie showed him some moves, like hand and arm strikes, punches, and kicking techniques. She did a side kick and a front kick to the garden table. She was so strong that the table flew at least a couple hundred yards in the air.

Emilie, embarrassed, said, "Oops!"

Tom said, "Wow! I've never seen anyone with so much strength!"

Cody said, "You should see her throw some dragons around! She threw me all the way to Emerald Forest with one hand. It was so much fun!"

"What? Throw Cody?" said Tom.

Emilie said, "No, no, Cody, I see that smile on your face, and I'm not going to do that right now. Besides, we've got a lot to do today." She turned to Tom and said, "Are you ready for another adventurous day?"

Tom, excited, said, "Yes, what are we doing today?"

Emilie said, "We'll visit Jane Peacock. She's invited us to her gardens for a tea party. Look at this fancy scroll invitation. Harry the Hedgehog dropped it by this morning. Here, read it." Emilie handed the scroll to Tom.

The scroll was very beautiful and ornate with carved wooden

handles on each end. It was made of thick parchment paper. The back of it was decorated with drawings of colorful peacock feathers, and it was lined with tinges of silver foil. Tom unraveled the scroll and read it aloud.

"TO: Emilie, Nala, Cody, and Tom
FROM: Jane Peacock

Dear Fellow Azarians and Tom,
I, Jane Peacock, would like to invite you all for a fabulous afternoon tea party in my beautiful gardens. The tea party will promptly start at 2pm, and do not be late! Please respond below.

Signed,
Jane Peacock
Fine Tailor & Gardener Extraordinaire

RSVP ASAP:

Say 'Yes' to accept this invitation.

Say 'No' to decline the invitation. (And I hope you do not decline this invitation because I'll be terribly disappointed!)"

Tom read the RSVP part again, puzzled. He gave the scroll back to Emilie.

She read it and said to the scroll, "Yes, Jane, we will be there promptly at two p.m., and we won't be late!" The scroll lifted in the air and rolled itself up. Wings appeared at its edges, and it flew off to Jane Peacock to tell her they would be coming to her fabulous tea party.

Tom, in disbelief, said, "Were those wings? That invitation just flew away!"

Emilie said, "Why, yes, I mean, she has to know if we are coming or not, right? Oh, and also, we can't be late. Jane is a little obsessed with being on time."

Cody said, "A little obsessed? You mean a lot obsessed!"

Tom said, "Why? What will happen if we're late?"

Nala said, "She will bite your head off! But don't worry, we won't be late."

Tom said, with worry, "Bite my head off?"

Nala said, "No, she won't bite your head off, Tom, she'll bite Cody's head off." Nala winked at him with a sly smile on his face. Tom nervously laughed and hoped Nala was indeed joking.

They got ready and took off. Emilie said to Tom, "Jane Peacock lives farther inland, so we need to fly there to make it in time for the tea party. We'll make a quick stop to see our friends the Wuzzlies, who live right by Jane."

Tom said, "The Wuzzlies? Who are the Wuzzlies?"

Emilie said, "You'll find out soon enough!"

Cody started to descend next to a field full of brightly colored poppies. Popping colors of red and orange blanketed the land. They landed and walked along a trail.

Emilie said, "The Wuzzlies live here next to the poppy fields, and Jane lives just over the bridge about a half mile down. Tom, I wanted to tell you about the Wuzzlies. They are just the cutest things! Now, don't be alarmed if they—"

Tom interrupted Emilie, as he saw something coming up fast behind her. "What is that white ball rolling on the ground over there? A tumbleweed of some kind? It's coming really fast and—"

The white ball of fur was so quick, it took Tom by surprise. Before he knew it, the white furball had rolled up and clung to the bottom of his leg. He screamed and tried to shake it off, but the big ball of fur held on tightly. He shook and shook his leg, but it didn't budge. Then the white ball of fur started to giggle loudly.

Emilie, Nala, and Cody laughed hysterically.

Emilie said, still laughing, "Tom, calm down! It's a Wuzzly! Stop shaking your leg, or he'll never let go! He just likes you. He's actually welcoming you!"

Tom was on the ground screaming and shaking his leg in the air. He turned to Emilie, sat up, and said, "What, this is a Wuzzly?" He stood up, out of breath, while the Wuzzly still hung on giggling.

Emilie walked to the Wuzzly on Tom's leg, bent down, pointed her finger at it, and said, "Now, Fibby Wuzzly, you can't just cling on to our visitor like that. You scared him! Get down from his leg this instant and say hello to Tom."

Fibby Wuzzly said in a little, sweet, sorrowful voice, "Sorry,

Emilie, I'll come down." Fibby let go and rolled down to the ground.

Wuzzlies were adorable creatures that looked like little white fluffy balls of fur. They were two feet round but stood four feet tall with their skinny legs extended. They had little eyes, ears, noses, and mouths. They also had long, skinny arms with small hands that hung down on the sides and long, skinny legs with tiny feet. They had very long, lush, black, adorable eyelashes that batted at creatures or visitors whenever they were in trouble or wanted something. They loved to roll and bounce very high. When they rolled, their hands and feet retracted, and their bodies formed white balls of fur that could reach very high speeds. They showed their affection by hugging or "clinging on" to creatures or visitors. They also loved to dance and sing, especially in front of visitors.

Fibby rolled down to the ground with his arms and skinny, long legs extended. His nose and other features were now visible, as the white fur around his face had receded to show the cute little creature fully.

Fibby stood in front of Tom, batted his long eyelashes, and sadly said, "Sorry, Tom, I didn't mean to scare you."

Tom looked at Fibby and felt bad. He knelt down and said, "It's all right, little fella. I was just surprised. I hope I didn't hurt you trying to shake you off my leg."

Fibby exclaimed, "No, it was fun! Can we do it again?!" Fibby's face lit up with a big smile.

Emilie said, "Fibby, I don't think Tom liked that. Did you, Tom?" She looked at Tom, and he quickly shook his head. "Cody and Nala will be happy to play with you later. But where are the others?"

"I'll go get them!" Fibby turned back into a furball and swiftly rolled away.

Nala said, "Seems like he likes you, Tom. Keep your eyes out because they are really fast!"

Suddenly, balls of white fur came rolling and bouncing around the poppy field at high speed. Before Tom could move aside and hide behind Cody, the Wuzzlies had rolled up and covered every part of Tom except his face. He was completely covered in white fur and stood with his hands straight out to his sides like a stick man. He couldn't move and had a worried look on his face.

Nala, Cody, and Emilie laughed hysterically.

Tom said in a little voice, "Help."

Nala said to Tom, "Looks like you've been Wuzzled!"

Tom said, "What? Wuzzled?"

Nala continued, "Yes, meaning that you are covered with Wuzzlies. They only do that if they really like you!"

Emilie said, still laughing, "You look like that snowman! What is his name? Oh yeah, the Abominable Snowman!"

They all laughed, and the Wuzzlies hung on and giggled.

Emilie said, "Okay, Wuzzlies, let's leave Tom alone! Come down and introduce yourselves."

The Wuzzlies rolled down and stood in front of Tom. There were eight of them, and they looked up at Tom and batted their long, lush eyelashes. Tom smiled, as these were the cutest creatures he had ever seen. He thought, *How could anyone ever get mad or upset at such adorable faces as these?*

Emilie said, "Wuzzlies, this is Tom, our visitor."

All the Wuzzlies lined up and introduced themselves one by one.

"I am Fibby Wuzzly, the one that clung on your leg first!"

"I am Fuzzy."

"I am Dibby."

"I am Buzzy."

They all giggled before the others continued.

"I am Doozi."

"And I am Ziggy."

"I am Suzie."

"And I am Pipsi Wuzzly."

They all smiled and looked at Tom and batted their long eyelashes.

He said, "Well, nice to meet you Fibby, uh, Fuzzy. No, you're Fuzzy, and you're Buzzy? Umm, well, nice to meet you all!"

The Wuzzlies giggled and looked at each other.

Emilie said, "We are on our way to Jane Peacock. We wanted to drop by and say hello and for you to meet Tom."

Buzzy Wuzzly said, "Will Tom be at the big festival?"

Tom said, "What festival?"

Emilie said, "Yes, he'll be there, Buzzy." She turned to Tom and said, "It's the Annual Festival of Azar. It's the biggest celebration on Azar with lots of food, games, dancing, and music. It's the day before you leave, so you'll be here to enjoy the festivities."

They continued down the path to Jane Peacock's house. The Wuzzlies rolled and bounced around and had a marvelous time giggling and marching down the poppy fields. They then started to dance in a circle and sing the Wuzzly song:

"We are the Wuzzlies, we love to fool around.
We ziggle and zaggle
And giggle and gaggle
And figgle and faggle!
We're faster than light!
Rolling, big balls of white!
We're the Wuzzlies from Azar!

We are the Wuzzlies, we love to bounce around.
Now don't you forget
And watch where your step
Cuz you'll deeply regret
Stepping on a Wuzzly from Azar!

We are the Wuzzlies, we love to dance around.
So get on your feet
And dance to this beat
Cuz you're in for a treat!
We're the Wuzzlies from Azar!

We ziggle and zaggle
And giggle and gaggle
And figgle and faggle!
We run at top speed!
So if you see us, please heed!
We're the wonderful...Wuzzlies...from...Azaaar!"

Everyone clapped, and the Wuzzlies took a bow.

Emilie said, "Oh, look! There's the bridge straight ahead. We're almost there."

A few minutes later, they reached the edge of the bridge. Emilie turned to the Wuzzlies and said, "Okay, my cute little friends, we have to go now. We'll see you all at the festival next week!"

The Wuzzlies stood in front of them looking very sad. They batted their long eyelashes, waved goodbye, and rolled away into the poppy fields.

Everyone else crossed the bridge and walked down a road lined with neatly trimmed green shrubs. A big house sat at the end of the road. At the corner across the house was an apple tree.

They stopped at the tree, and Emilie said, "This is Harry the Hedgehog's house. Let's see if he's home."

It was a very large apple tree with many red, ripe apples hanging from it. The tree had a large trunk with a red door on the bottom and a window with a windowsill full of daisies on the top. A welcome sign hung just above the door.

Emilie knocked on the door to see if Harry was home.

Seconds later, Harry popped his head out of the window above and said, "Hello, everyone! I'll be right down." The front door opened, and it was Harry the Hedgehog wearing a purple-and-black checkered coat with a purple bow tie. Harry said, "Welcome, my friends! You are just in time, as I was headed out to Jane's place. We can walk together."

Emilie said, "Great, let's get going! We don't want to be late for Jane's tea party. By the way, you look really nice, Harry."

Nala said, "Very snazzy, Harry!"

Cody said, "Very chic, Harry, very chic!"

Harry said, "Thank you. Jane wanted us to match at the tea party, so she made this for me this morning when your RSVP flew in. She is all about matching and fashion!"

They reached Jane Peacock's house, which was encompassed within a beautiful front garden. Hedges shaped in whimsical patterns ran along the edges of the large rectangular area. A big, three-tiered water fountain was on the left, and a large green topiary shrub shaped like a peacock was on the right. They walked up the steps and stood in front of a huge dome-shaped door. The front door was made of thick, dark wood in which peacock feathers were carved.

Harry said, "Go on in, the door is open."

Nala pushed the giant door, and it opened into an enormous entranceway full of clocks. Big clocks, small clocks, round clocks, square clocks, and triangular clocks of all different colors covered the entire room, including the ceiling.

There was one clock that stood out from the rest, as it was the biggest and most impressive clock in the room. It was a grandfather clock that was twenty feet tall and sat right across the door. It was made of rich, dark brown wood and had a gold face with a gold pendulum swinging back and forth.

Tom walked through the door and looked around. He looked up toward the ceiling and said in astonishment, "I've never seen so many clocks in one room!" He looked at the grandfather clock and admired the beauty and craftsmanship of it.

Harry said, "There are exactly one thousand clocks from floor to ceiling. Ever since we had the Dutch clockmaker visit us, she has been obsessed with clocks and time, as you can see. He made the grandfather clock for Jane as a gift."

Harry went over to the gigantic grandfather clock, floated up, looked at the time, and said, "Oh, good, we have fifteen minutes till Grandfather strikes two. Let's make our way to the gardens, shall we?"

Everyone followed Harry. When they passed the grandfather clock, they all said hello to it.

First, Nala said, "Hello, Grandfather!"

Then Emilie and Cody said, "Hi, Grandfather!"

A face of a pleasant and smiling old man materialized on the clock, and he said, "Hello, everyone! Welcome to Jane Peacock's humble abode! And who do we have here?"

Tom was shocked at first that the clock talked, but he quickly calmed down and took it quite well. Since the rose tree incident, he was getting used to the idea of trees and now furniture talking.

Tom said, "Hello, Grandfather. My name is Tom."

Grandfather Clock said, "Ahhh, the visitor! Jane said such nice things about you. Pleased to meet you, Tom. Why don't you all go on in and make yourself at home?"

They all said bye to Grandfather Clock and continued to a hallway that had pictures of fellow Azarians hanging on the walls. Tom saw one of Harry the Hedgehog and Bakari the Emperor Cat and a very pretty picture of Emilie smiling in a blue dress.

Tom waved Cody and Nala over and pointed at Emilie's picture. Emilie peeked over their shoulders and said, "Yes, that's me. Theodore painted that. Theodore does most of the paintings here."

Tom looked at Bakari's picture for a moment and thought even in a painting, Bakari looked frightening smiling back at him with his huge fangs. He jumped as he saw something move. *Did he just wink at me?* Tom wondered. He looked at Bakari's painting again, and nothing moved. He shook his head and continued on.

They entered another room with cathedral-like vaulted ceilings. The room was very large, and the ceilings were painted with pretty pictures of flowers and birds on a background of a blue sky. This was where Jane Peacock worked. There were trundles of threads and boxes of buttons, strings of pearls, and brightly colored beads in one corner of the room. Rolls and rolls of beautiful, colorful fabric were stacked in another corner, and several sewing machines along the windows looked out to the garden. A big working table in the middle of the room was covered with tape measures, colorful feathers, cut-up patterns of what seemed to be a dinner jacket in the making, and a hat half covered in gemstones and feathers. Harry waved everyone to the outside garden.

They stepped outside into a colorful flower garden that was absolutely stunning. Roses, marigolds, tulips, peonies, lilies, and other flowers were sectioned off by neatly trimmed hedges. An arbor of pink climbing roses sat in the corner covering an outdoor seating area. Butterflies fluttered about, and a heavenly scent of flowers filled the air.

What was even more spectacular was the garden beyond this flower garden…it was like stepping into the Gardens of Versailles. It contained a vast collection of meticulously manicured lawns shaped in ornate designs. A tall water fountain of a dozen blue dolphins stood in the middle surrounded by rows of red and orange peonies. On the far end was a large hedge maze.

Tom couldn't believe how beautiful it was here. He hadn't expected this at all.

Emilie said, "A couple hundred years ago, we had a visitor from France. He was a gardener and a genius at designing gardens. He loved Azar's vegetation and different species of flowers and shrubbery that were not found in his world. He and Jane worked on these gardens together. The gardens are vast, and you can get lost in them quite easily, especially in that maze there. It is all truly a masterpiece."

Grandfather Clock loudly struck two o'clock. Jane Peacock came walking down the path to greet them. Jane was elegantly dressed in a purple, velvet dress trimmed in gold with gold buttons. She wore a matching hat embellished with purple stones and gold feathers.

She said, "Hello, my friends, welcome to my home! I'm sure you are all famished from your journey. Let's go to the flower garden and have some tea and refreshments."

They walked back to the flower garden, and there stood a long, elegant table dressed in white linen. Purple, iridescent plates, cups, and saucers etched in gold along with matching silverware were laid out on the table. Pink and green floral centerpieces, freshly picked from Jane's gardens, were displayed at the ends of the table. A feast of fruits, pies, breads, and the delicacies of Azar were laid out. Trays of treats displayed cookies, biscuits, chocolates shaped as little birds and butterflies, and scones filled with dragonberry jam. Teapots, teacups, and saucers painted with pink flowers were set out to serve delicious, fragrant tea. A real feast was before their eyes.

Everyone looked at all the goodies and licked their lips. Cody and Nala were the first to sit and be ready to eat, each with a knife and fork in their hands and a white linen napkin tied behind their necks.

Emile said, "Everything looks great, Jane!"

Harry started to pour tea into everyone's cups.

Jane Peacock said, "Dig in, everyone!"

They did just that, everyone devouring the food in silence. They finished eating and were stuffed. Cody and Nala went off to the side and lay down on the grass, ready to take their usual naps.

Jane Peacock said, "Would you like to see my new gardening project?"

Tom and Emilie nodded and quickly finished their tea. Harry joined them as they walked along a different pathway lined with green cypress trees. At the end of the pathway was a pond lined with shimmering blue stones and with a waterfall in the middle. Lily pads and white lotus flowers floated on the surface. Four large swans swam in the waters. A slight breeze blew smells of jasmine through the air.

Jane Peacock said, "This is my new project. I call it the Flower Arches. It's divided into sections with arches of different flowers. We have the jasmine arches here. The smell is just divine, isn't it?"

They walked under the jasmine arches, which led to a circular garden that surrounded a small fountain. Seats and benches shaped like butterflies and birds were situated on the far end.

Tom said, "The gardens are beautiful, Jane. Emilie said you had a visitor from France that helped you with the gardens?"

Jane Peacoock said, "Yes, he was brilliant and so much fun to work with. He taught me about landscaping and design and which flowers and shrubs to use in different displays. It was a learning lesson for all of us. You see, Tom, we love when visitors come to Azar. They teach us marvelous things that we incorporate into our daily lives. In fact, one of my favorite visitors—aside from you, Tom," she winked at him, "—was an opera singer from Italy. He was a maestro of opera and could carry a note that would give you chills. He gave us Azarians a little concert before he left that I will never forget. He even taught Cody and I how to sing opera. In fact, we'll be performing a duet together at the festival next week."

"Really?" Tom asked. "I love opera. I'm looking forward to it!"

Jane Peacock laughed and said, "Oh, he was such a kind gentleman, and, boy, did he love to eat! I've never met a human that ate so much dragonberry pie! I think he gained at least ten pounds in the days he was here."

They laughed and walked back to the house.

As they approached the flower garden, a large bird flew overhead. It was Theodore the Great Owl.

Jane Peacock said, "Well, what a surprise, it's Theodore! Are you crashing my tea party, Theodore?" Jane Peacock smiled, and

Theodore laughed. She continued, "Oh, I'm just joking, Theodore. Here, have some tea and taste some of my freshly made treats."

Theodore tasted the treats and said, "My, my, Jane, these are very good. I actually came by to try on my jacket for the festival. You said it was ready?"

Jane said, "Oh, yes, let me go see. I think I may need to make a small adjustment on it."

Harry, Jane, and Emilie walked back to the house.

Theodore took a sip of his tea and said to Tom, "So tell me, Tom, how are you enjoying your stay?"

Tom said, "It's actually very nice. I just need to get used to flying everywhere and also things talking like trees and clocks, but so far, it's been amazing."

Theodore laughed and said, "Ah, yes, it's a shock at first, but you'll get used to it. Emilie said you saw the unicorns yesterday?"

Tom said, "Yes, I met the unicorns. They are beautiful creatures like everything here—beautiful and carefree."

Theodore continued sipping his tea.

Tom continued, "It's different here in a good way. It's refreshing to be in a natural and laid-back environment away from the daily traffic and congestion—the everyday hustle and bustle, as we call it. What's really great is that I haven't had any asthma symptoms since I've been here. What a relief from using my inhaler almost every day thanks to the clean air here in Azar!"

Theodore said, "Yes, Emilie had mentioned your discussion earlier about pollution in the air. I do know a little about what goes on in your world. Pollution in your environment seems to make the news often. We Azarians are pretty much self-sufficient creatures, and that is why our world is so beautiful and untouched. I understand that humans depend on vehicles for transportation, and big factories produce human necessities, but perhaps there is something that could be done."

Tom said, "Yes, I had mentioned that to Emilie, and she seems to think that I can do something about it. It's an impossible feat for one person to tackle given the magnitude of the problem. It would have to take a collective effort from many, many people to make a change, as there are a lot of factors involved."

Theodore paused and said, "Ah, yes, but look at these gardens in front of you. Only one human and one Azarian worked together to make this magnificent spectacle. You know, Tom, humans are very intelligent creatures. I mean, you found a way to fly to the moon, which is most impressive considering you have no wings or magical powers. I'm sure you will figure it out one day."

Tom said, "I hope we do."

They continued to drink their tea. Tom contemplated every word the wise owl had said. He then said, "Just curious, but how do you know what goes on in my world?"

Theodore smiled. "Why, my magic crystal ball, of course."

Tom smiled back and said, "Of course, your magic crystal ball."

They both returned to their tea while looking out at the majestic gardens displayed in front of them.

Jane came out and said, "Theodore, the jacket is all done. Come in here and try it on."

Emilie said, "We better get going, Tom, we have a big day ahead of us tomorrow."

Theodore said, "Tom, it was nice chatting with you. Enjoy the rest of your time here on Azar, and I will see you at my home in the Emerald Forest in a couple days."

Everyone said farewell to Jane Peacock and Harry the Hedgehog and thanked them for their wonderful hospitality.

Jane said to Tom, "I'll see you at the festival, Tom. Enjoy your time with Bakari tomorrow. Don't you worry now, he is just a little pussycat!"

They took off on Cody.

Worried, Tom asked, "Did she say that we are seeing Bakari tomorrow?"

Emilie nodded and said, "Yup. Don't worry, Bakari doesn't bite!"

Emilie, Nala, and Cody laughed while Tom cringed at the thought of Bakari taking a big bite out of him.

DAY 5
BAKARI THE EMPEROR CAT

TOM WOKE UP READY FOR ANOTHER ADVENTUROUS day. He went for his usual morning swim, got dressed, groomed himself, and headed to the breakfast table. He walked down the hallway and heard a sound coming from the room in back. He turned around, saw the door slightly ajar, and slowly crept to the door. He poked his head around the doorway and saw an enormous tree standing in the middle of the room.

He entered the room and looked around. No one was in sight. There was also no furniture, or ceiling, for that matter, as this tree was mammoth in height. The tree had a thick trunk and sturdy branches with needle-like, flat green leaves. It reminded him of the giant redwood trees he saw back home on hiking trips with his friends.

Tom thought to himself, *Why would a tree be in this room?*

He heard a rustling coming from above followed by a dark, fathomless growl that sent chills down his spine. It seemed something large was swiftly coming down the tree. Tom was frightened and quickly backed up against the wall. The large creature reached the bottom then jumped off the tree and landed with a big thump, shaking the ground beneath them. Tom screamed and looked at the creature that towered over him; it was Nala smiling down at him.

Tom quickly came to his senses and said, "Nala! This is your room? Why is this tree here?"

Nala said, "I don't sleep on beds like you and Emilie do. I would rather sleep on a comfy branch way up there where the stars shine at night. Besides, it's fun going up and down and good exercise, too. And my tree is magical. In the morning, it transforms and wakes me up. It's kinda like an alarm clock. Take a look."

Nala and Tom looked up toward the sky. The room became brighter, and the sun began to shine down upon them. The tree started to produce many little buds that grew into pretty, light pink flowers.

Tom said, "What a nice way to wake up in the morning. I wouldn't mind sleeping up in the tree one night with you. Looks like it would be fun up there."

Nala, with a puzzled look on his face, said, "Really? I don't think you would like it up there. There are no soft leaves like you and Emilie have on your beds. Plus, you might fall off the branch in the middle of the night and plummet to your death."

Tom gulped and said, "Good point. I think I'll sleep on my comfortable bed of leaves."

Nala laughed and said, "Let's go have some breakfast."

They both walked down the hallway and headed to the kitchen. Emilie knocked on the window and waved them over to come outside. They went outside where breakfast was waiting on the table, as was Cody with knife and fork in hand ready to eat.

Emilie said, "We have a big day ahead of us, so let's eat!"

They sat down, and everyone noticed Tom wasn't his usual talkative, happy self this morning. He knew they were going to see Bakari and dreaded the thought of spending a whole day with the emperor cat.

Emilie said, "Ready to meet Bakari?"

Tom took a deep breath and said gloomily, "Yes, as ready as I'll ever be."

Emilie said, "Relax, Tom. Every time I mention Bakari, you have this sour look on your face. I think by the end of the day, you two will be the best of friends!"

Emilie, Cody, and Nala laughed.

Tom said, without any excitement, "I doubt that. But I'm ready to go and get this over with."

They took off and headed to Pinnacle Mountain where Bakari lived.

They flew over the rose trees of Azar. Their flowers were yellow this morning.

Emilie looked down and shouted, "Hello, Mr. Rose, I see you are all bright and yellow today. Looks wonderful!"

Mr. Rose looked up, smiled, and waved back.

Emilie turned to Tom and said, "I think it's about time you flew solo with Cody from now on."

Tom said, "By myself?"

Cody said, "Don't worry, Tom, I won't let anything happen to you. Besides, Nala is right next to us," Nala smiled and waved to Tom, "and Emilie will be on the other side. Trust me, it's a much better view flying alone."

Emilie turned to Tom and said, "You should move up here."

Emilie stood up and flew to the side. Tom scooted to the front of Cody. He did like flying by himself, and the view was much better than sitting behind a fairy with large wings. He gave a thumbs up to Emilie and Nala, and they continued on to Pinnacle Mountain.

Minutes after Emilie said, "We're almost there," a magnificent castle sitting atop a steep mountain came into view.

They descended and landed at the bottom of a hill surrounded by green shrubs arranged in neat lines. They walked up a path and were almost at the foot of the mountain when Tom stumbled on a rock and fell next to a green shrub full of colorful fruit. He looked closely at the many dangling fruits. They looked exactly like big, plump strawberries, but in an array of colors like pink, red, green, blue, orange, yellow, and purple.

Tom asked Emilie, "Are these strawberries?"

Emilie said, "Yes, they are strawberries. They come in all different colors."

Tom said, "Wow! We only have red where I'm from. I've never seen strawberries that are blue or purple. Do the colors mean they taste different?"

Emilie said, "No, they taste the same. Try one. It's very good."

Tom tasted a pink strawberry, then a purple and green one, and said, "Delicious." He continued to stuff his mouth when suddenly there was a loud *ROAR!* They all turned around to find three angry empress cats staring at Tom.

Empress cats were the female counterparts of the emperor cat and had the same majestic features as the emperor. They possessed beautiful manes that encircled their heads, black shiny coats, long tails, and elegant wings. The female had a smaller face, a slightly smaller body, and was shorter in length than the male. The empress cat might appear to have gentle and refined features but were more fearsome and vicious than their male counterparts when agitated.

"Who are you that is eating our fruit?" an empress cat exclaimed.

Tom was terrified, and with a mouthful of strawberries, started to choke.

Emilie quickly went to his side and said, "Are you all right?"

He coughed and coughed.

The empress cats approached them, and one said, "I think this human is choking. Would you like me to stick my paw down his throat and get it out?"

Tom shook his head and clutched his throat with both hands.

Emilie quickly placed her hand on his back and gave him several blows between his shoulder blades.

It worked, as Tom stopped choking and swallowed. He took a deep breath, stood up straight, and said to Emilie, "Thank you." He turned to the empress cats and said, "I'm sorry for eating your fruit, I just wanted to taste them."

Emilie said, "It's okay, Tom. They didn't know who you were, and now they do. Tom, this is Dahlia the Empress Cat, and this is Zania and Danube."

Dahlia said, "I apologize. I didn't mean to scare you. Bakari has instructed us to take you to the top. He is waiting for us all. Get on my back, and I will take you up there."

Tom gulped and worriedly said, "On your back? Uhh, I can ride on Cody. I mean, not that I don't want to ride with you, but I, umm…."

Dahlia chuckled and said, "Why, of course, I understand. We will see you all up there."

The empress cats spread their beautiful wings and flew to the top of the mountain. Everyone followed and landed in front of a huge fortified castle with several towers and turrets made of black rock that gleamed in the light. A long red carpet extended to the castle's front doors. The empress cats ran into the castle, and Emilie, Nala, Cody, and Tom walked the red carpet. They reached the castle steps and stood in front of two massive, dome-shaped wooden doors that were wide open. On each door hung a shiny gold door knocker shaped like an emperor cat's head. As they walked through the doors, the eyes on the door knockers turned into real eyes that watched Tom's every move.

They entered the castle, and along the entrance walls were pictures of fellow Azarians. Tom saw a picture of the cute Wuzzlies lined up that brought a smile to his face. He was looking at a picture of Theodore the Owl when he heard a giggle. Tom thought it sounded like a Wuzzly giggling. He looked around then back at the Wuzzlies picture. He stared at it for a minute then placed his ear next to it and listened. He heard nothing, shook his head, and moved on.

They walked into a giant room filled with tables and chairs made of the same black rock as on the castle's exterior walls.

Tom stood in the center of the room and looked up at the towering ceiling, which must have been one hundred feet in height, and there hung an enormous chandelier. The chandelier was bright gold and stunning. It contained hundreds of lit candles that sat atop delicately swooping, fluted arms dressed in crystal prism drops, which sparkled in the light. The walls were adorned with rich, colorful tapestries of Azar's beautiful scenery, including Jane Peacock's majestic gardens.

Toward the back were stairs that led up to a large platform on which a throne stood. The throne was exquisite and made of gold. Two emperor cats were carved into the bottom legs, and the seat was covered in tufted red velvet with a black trim. It was magnificent and befitting of royalty. It was where Bakari sat.

The empress and emperor cats were lined up on the stairs, surrounding the room, and standing guard at the front doors. There must have been at least a couple hundred of the majestic creatures waiting for their leader.

As they stood in the middle of the room waiting, Emilie said to Tom, "Bakari is coming."

Bakari appeared at the top of a long spiral staircase behind the platform. He quickly ran down and walked to his throne. He sat down and gave a big *ROAR!* He then looked at his guests and said, "Welcome, my friends, to Pinnacle Mountain! Tom, I see you have made it in one piece." Bakari laughed and continued, "Dahlia said you choked on our fruit. Is this correct?"

Tom nervously said, "Um, yes, your emperorship. I mean, Emperor Bakari, sir."

Bakari jumped down from his throne and slowly walked up to the frightened human. Standing in front of him, he sniffed Tom and said, "My dear Tom, I can smell fear on you, and I do not know why. I am not such a bad cat, am I? In fact, you can ask any of my fellow cats standing here, and they will say what a great emperor I am. What have I done that makes you so fearful of me? Do you not remember our conversation at the Council about Golden Rule Number One?"

Tom nodded.

Bakari said, "Good, now do you remember what we had said about Azarians not harming or eating humans?"

Tom nodded and said, "Yes, I do remember that."

Bakari continued and said sincerely, "I would never violate what we agreed upon at the Council. My word is my honor!" Bakari placed his right paw over his heart. "Now, let us be friends and have some food and drink to celebrate your arrival! What do you say?"

Tom felt a rush of relief. He felt that what Bakari had said was genuine and from the heart. "Okay. Yes, let us celebrate."

Bakari smiled and said, "Wonderful! Come, I have prepared a feast for you all!"

They entered another room that was lavishly decorated in gold and red tones. A long table with a red velvet runner down the middle and chairs made of black rock sat in the center of the room. Gold bowls, plates, saucers, and matching utensils were laid out elegantly. Many delicacies of Azar were displayed along with bowls of the strawberries that grew plentifully outside the castle grounds.

Bakari sat at the head of the table and said to Tom, "Come sit next to me. I had them prepare bowls of strawberries for you since

I heard you devoured them earlier." Bakari raised his eyebrow and placed a bowl in front of him.

Tom laughed and plopped one in his mouth.

Bakari said, "My friends, please eat up!"

The empress cats poured a pink bubbly liquid into everyone's cups. Bakari raised his cup and made a toast. "To my friend Tom. May he continue to enjoy the beauties of Azar!"

They all raised their cups and drank. Bakari, Cody, and Nala downed their drinks in one gulp, licked their lips, and were ready for more.

Tom took a sip and was delighted by the taste. He said, "Wow, what is this drink called? It's refreshing, and it has a tingling sensation to it."

Bakari said, "Ah, you like it, I see. It's called the mambo mimosa! It has the berries that you like and some other things mixed in."

"Mambo mimosa? I like it!" Tom said.

He took another sip, and Emilie whispered to him, "Take it easy on that, Tom, it's kinda like dragon beer. Remember you and dragon beer the first day here?"

He remembered he had passed out on the kitchen table and woken up the next day in his bed. Tom was glad Emilie had warned him because he wouldn't want to pass out at Bakari's table. It would be rude and a definite no-no!

They continued to enjoy the feast and drank more mambo mimosas. Nala and Cody went off to the side as usual and took a nap by the red velvet couches. Emilie talked with Zania and Dahlia about the festival coming up.

Bakari said to Tom, "Did you really think I would ever harm you?"

Tom was feeling really good due to the mambo mimosas. He felt at ease with Bakari and that he could open up to him. He casually said, "Yes, you looked pretty scary to me when I first saw you at the Council. You also have these big, humongous fangs," he pointed to Bakari's fangs, "that look like they could slice me in half in a second."

Bakari laughed with his enormous mouth open wide, and Tom stared at his white fangs. Tom laughed as well.

Bakari said, "You know, Tom, I have not harmed any creature or visitor in the 10,537 years of my life. But then the portal opened to other planets, and there was one time I had a want to use my big humongous fangs on someone, but I did not! You see, this visitor from your world called himself a poacher. Do you know what a poacher is?"

Tom nodded, listening intently.

Bakari continued, "Well, having a poacher here on Azar is like, as you would say, 'having a kid in a candy shop.' In fact, the first time I met him at the Council, I could only smell death coming from him, and my nose never lies. I didn't like him from the start, and none of the creatures of Azar wanted to be around him. One night, he snuck away from Emilie and Nala's home, and, well, let's just say he departed Azar unexpectedly."

Tom, concerned, said, "What happened to this visitor?"

Bakari had a big sly smile on his face when he said, "You may want to ask Theodore himself, as he took care of him personally. Don't let his innocent little owl looks fool you. Theodore has no mercy for violators of the Golden Rules, and nor do I or any Azarian, for that matter!"

Tom said, "I don't blame you for protecting the creatures of Azar. I would do the same thing. Poaching is illegal in my world, but unfortunately, it is still going on. It's a billion-dollar business driven by consumer demand. In fact, it threatens many species with extinction, like the African elephants, who are killed for their ivory. The black rhinos are so few now and in danger of becoming extinct because many people believe that their horns have some medicinal effect to cure the sick. This theory has been scientifically proven wrong, and it's heartbreaking that they are being eliminated for medicines that don't work. Other animals, like the tiger, cheetah, leopards, and gorillas, may become extinct in the next decade, not only because of poaching, but because of other factors like habitat destruction and climate change. I don't like it at all, what they do to these poor, defenseless animals, but it is a big problem in our world."

Bakari said, "That is unfortunate to hear. If it is illegal, then why is it still going on? Do you humans not obey the laws? If a human broke the law here, they would end up like our poacher friend—bye-bye." Bakari waved "*bye-bye*" with his paw.

Tom said, "It's very different in my world, Bakari. You can't just say 'bye-bye' to them. There is a lot of money to be made in poaching, and we don't have the resources to address the problem properly. I mean, there are some organizations around the world trying to end animal poaching, but I don't know if they can thoroughly eliminate it. I believe consumers—the people that buy the animal products—are the key to ending these heartless killings."

Bakari said, "You seem knowledgeable about the subject. Perhaps you can think of a way to save these innocent animals."

Tom said, "I am just one person, Bakari. What can I do?"

Bakari said, "A lot, I would think. Don't underestimate yourself, Tom. I can see the spark and passion in your eyes. Well, let us not worry about that right now. I'm sure you humans will figure things out one day." Bakari smiled. "Come now, we must continue our celebration! Come walk with me, Tom."

Tom stood up, and Bakari placed his giant paw around Tom's

shoulder and walked with him. Bakari's paw was so heavy that it threw Tom off balance. He struggled to stay standing and kept walking and limping as best he could.

Bakari said, "I like you, Tom, so I want to show you something special that no visitor has ever set their eyes on. It's just out here through the balcony."

Cody and Nala awakened from their naps and followed them out onto the balcony. Emilie and the empress cats also followed.

They walked down the balcony steps, and in front of them were green shrubs that sparkled in the sunlight.

Bakari said, "Behold, the golden fruit!"

The shrubs, lined up in rows, were gleaming with dots of gold. Tom took a closer look at the golden fruit. They were beautiful, plump, golden strawberries.

Bakari said to everyone, "Have a taste, my friends!"

Everyone proceeded to their own bush and tasted the succulent golden fruit. Tom picked one, plopped it into his mouth, and smiled contentedly. He thought it tasted amazing. It was the sweetest, most delicious berry he had ever had, and he immediately felt a sense of happiness go through him that he couldn't explain.

He turned to Cody and Nala, and they, too, were devouring the scrumptious fruit.

Bakari came to Tom and said, "You see, my friend, these are magical fruit, and they only grow here on Pinnacle Mountain outside my beautiful castle. We take the golden fruit, and we make a concoction that will blow your mind. Since I like you, I will let you taste the golden liquid. Come, everyone! We will drink the Emperor's Roar!"

The emperor and empress cats lit up with joy at the mention of the Emperor's Roar. They quickly went inside to prepare for the special golden drink.

Tom asked Emilie, "What is the Emperor's Roar?"

Emilie said, "It is the golden liquid of the emperor cat, and you should be very happy because Bakari never ever brings the stuff out for visitors. The drink is delicious, but pace yourself, as it has a kick to it."

Tom nodded, excited to taste this golden liquid they were raving about. Everyone went back to the dining room and sat down.

Many emperor cats were standing around and seated with them at the table. As the empress cats carried trays of golden jugs with golden goblets into the dining room, the trumpets sounded, and the emperor and empress cats sang:

"Here it comes, the Emperor's Roar,
Lo and behold, it's the Emperor's Roar!

When Bakari commands, we stand and obey
He shouts, 'Bring out the liquid gold!'
Now stand aside and clear the way!

For here it comes, the Emperor's Roar,
Lo and behold, it's the Emperor's Roar!

A trickle of gold
A drop of delight
It's the drink to behold
At the end you just might

ROAR at the top of your lungs
ROAR! The celebration has begun
ROAR to the golden delight
It's the emperor's fruit that gleams in the light!

Here it comes, the Emperor's Roar,
All hail and behold, it's the Emperor's ROAR!"

They all raised their goblets, and Bakari made a toast, "To the Emperor's Roar!"

The emperor and empress cats drank their drinks in one gulp, slammed their goblets down, and belted out a big, *"ROAR!"* that shook the whole castle. They all laughed heartily and refilled their goblets.

Emilie, Nala, and Cody gulped their drinks as well and shouted, *"ROAR!"*

Tom took a big sip and was pleasantly surprised, as the silky golden liquid was so smooth. He could taste the berries, and it was simply exquisite. He said, "Delicious!" slammed the goblet down, and unintentionally belted out a big burp.

The others laughed out loud, and everyone again raised their goblets, guzzled down the golden liquid, slammed their goblets down, and belted out another big, *"ROAR!"* that shook the castle. They laughed and continued to celebrate through the night, talking mostly about the festival coming up in a few days.

Tom was having a grand time and enjoying his time with Bakari.

Emilie said to Tom, "See, I told you that you and Bakari would be good friends by the end of the day."

Tom smiled and had another sip of the Emperor's Roar. He was starting to see things out-of-focus and fuzzy.

Emilie knew it was time to go. They all thanked Bakari for a wonderful time and took off on Cody with Tom passed out all the way home.

DAY 6
MERIDIAN

TOM SLEPT IN AFTER THE NIGHT OF CELEBRATION with the emperor and empress cats. He realized he had been totally wrong about Bakari and was glad he had spent a day at Bakari's castle. It was the most fun he had had in years.

He got up and got dressed. He was starving after a night of celebration and roaring. In fact, his jaw still hurt because of it. He headed to the breakfast table and saw everyone outside doing their morning exercises. They were doing hard-core calisthenic training with push-ups, sit-ups, pull-ups, and jumping jacks.

He thought, *These creatures are really into their exercise, but push-ups and sit-ups are the last things I want to do.* The only thing on his mind was a stack of flapjacks drizzled with dragonberry syrup and a tall glass of Dragon's Delight.

He finished his breakfast and went outside. "Good morning. Do you guys exercise every morning?"

Nala said, "Of course. Gives us power! It's also a good way to start the day. Most Azarians do some form of exercise before they start the day. Don't you?"

Tom said, "Uhh, no. I'm just too busy with work. I really should start something when I get back home. Maybe I'll try surfing or paddle boarding since I live on the beach. I see many people doing it, and it looks like fun."

Cody asked, "What is surfing and paddle boarding? Can I try that?"

Tom laughed and said, "Well, Cody, I don't think a surfboard would be able to hold you up, you're just too heavy. Perhaps if they made surfboards for dragons, but I don't think that will work either because of the weight. But surfing is when you stand on an oblong, rectangular board and ride the waves. In paddle boarding, you stand up or kneel on the board while steering with a paddle. It's usually done on calm ocean waters. Now, that would be a sight to see—Cody the Dragon surfing the big waves!"

They all laughed.

Emilie said, "Speaking of waters and waves, I thought we'd spend the day with your saviors, the mermaids. Remember the mermaids from the first day of your arrival? They were the ones that rescued you and brought you to shore. You probably don't remember because you were unconscious when they picked you up."

Nala said, "Yup, very unconscious and practically almost dead."

Tom said, "Almost dead? All I remember was that I woke up on the beach and saw you guys and some giant seahorses with creatures on top of them. Those were mermaids on top? Everything was a blur."

Emilie said, "Yes, they were mermaids. They've invited us to their seahorse races today. It'll be a lot of fun, and all of Meridien will be there."

Tom said, excited, "Spend the day with mermaids? Heck yeah! This just gets better and better."

They took off and headed to the sea.

They landed on the white sand beaches of Azar. Tom recalled the last time he was on this beach frightened and running for his life. He thought, *What a complete turn of events from that day till now.* He looked toward the water and was astonished by what he saw.

Mermaids rode on giant seahorses, and an enormous octopus threw balls in the air with his many tentacles. Blue dolphins leapt high, caught the ball, and threw it back. Playful seals splashed around and joined in the ball game as well. There were also some very odd-looking sea creatures in the water. Fishes with neon pink scales, pink feathers fanning out around their heads, and full bright pink lips floated about. One looked at Tom, winked, and puckered its lips at him. There were also large fish with reptilian features. They had spiny scales under their chins and on top of their heads, fins on top of their bodies, bubbly eyes that protruded from their heads, and long tails that whipped around in the air.

Tom asked Nala, "What kind of fish is that one with the pink feathers, and also the other one over there that looks like a reptile?"

Nala said, "The ones with the pink feathers are called pink

pucker fish, and the other ones are dragon fish. It's half fish and half dragon. They can also walk on land. Here are a couple coming now."

The dragon fish swam to shore and started walking on four feet. They were five feet in length and stood two feet tall. They had pectoral fins on each side and gills to breathe underwater. They looked at Tom and said, "Hello, human!" Tom stared at these odd creatures and waved hello. The dragon fish lay on the sand and soaked up the sun's rays.

Oriana the Mermaid saw them and headed toward the shore along with five other mermaids on seahorses. They reached the beach and towered over them.

Emilie said, "Tom, I would like you to meet Oriana. She is the Queen of Meridien."

Oriana said, "Hello, Tom. You look much better than the last time I saw you. I'm glad you are doing well."

Tom didn't say a word, as he was mesmerized by the beauty of all of the mermaids before him. He thought the depictions of mermaids in storybooks were true except that they were more enchanting and beautiful in person. The mermaids had long, thick, and lustrous dark brown hair that hung all the way down to their waists. Their skin was light brown with a golden glow. They had iridescent blue fishtails from the waist down that changed color in the sunlight. They all wore golden leaf-like crowns embedded with little gold starfish and gold shells. Oriana's crown was larger with white pearls amongst the gold starfish, and she had a matching gold bracelet.

Emilie waved her hand in front of Tom's face, as he was unresponsive. "Tom? Tom? Are you there, Tom?"

He answered, "Sorry, it's just that I've only seen and read about you in storybooks, and to actually see you in person is surreal. You should know that many young girls adore you. Actually, many people throughout the world admire and love mermaids."

Oriana said, "That is really nice to hear. We are honored to know that we have such a following on Earth. Now, Tom, after the races, we can take you on a tour of Meridien so you can see how beautiful our underwater world is, if that is okay with you and your hosts?"

Emilie, Nala, and Cody nodded their heads and said, "Yup! No problem!"

Tom said, "That would be great, but there is one problem. I can't survive underwater for long periods of time. I could probably only hold my breath for one minute, but anything above that, I may pass out or even worse."

Emilie said, "Not to worry. I'll take care of that. Now let's sit back and watch the seahorse races!"

There were twelve pairs of mermaids on seahorses lined up by the shore ready to go. The giant octopus was off to the side and raised a blue flag.

Emilie said, "When the octopus lowers the flag, it means *go*. They must reach Blue Rock, which is a distance way. They are to go to Blue Rock, grab the flag of Meridien, race back to shore, and stick the flag into the sand. The first one that does that wins."

Cody said, "I think Sage the Seahorse will win. He is the fastest one here. He's the one riding with Oriana. There are two other seahorses who are worthy of the title, and that would be Morey on the far end and Shadow, the one next to him. Here we go, he is about to lower the flag."

And they were off! The seahorses jolted forward and left a wave of water behind them. Everyone cheered them on. Shadow took the lead with Morey in second, and Sage was in sixth place. After a short period of time, they were out of sight on their way toward Blue Rock. A few minutes later, they came back into view headed toward the finish line, each carrying a Meridien flag. The Meridien flag was blue with two white, wavy stripes that represented the waves of the water at the bottom and a yellow sun on the top right corner. Illustrations of a mermaid and two blue dolphins floated on the waves of water.

Nala said, "I can see them now. It looks like Shadow is in first place, and Sage is in second. Oh, wait a minute, coming up quickly behind Shadow is…is…Sage and Oriana! I think they're going to win!"

Sage sped to the finish line, and Oriana waved Meridien's flag up high, jumped down, stuck the flag in the sand, and won! Shadow was second, and Morey finished third. One after the other, they laid down the Meridien flag along the shore until there were twelve flags lined up on the sand. Everyone jumped up and down. They clapped and congratulated Sage and Oriana as well as the other participants on a job well done.

The festivities continued into the afternoon. Tom swam and played ball with the sea creatures for a while. He saw Cody along with the dragon fish on the sand sunbathing and decided to join them. He got out of the water, lay down next to the dragon fish, and enjoyed the sun's rays.

Emilie called Tom and waved him down to the shoreline. He got up and walked over. Emilie said, "Are you ready to explore Meridien?"

Tom excitedly said, "Yes, I'm ready, but how will I—"

Emilie waved her hand over Tom's head, and he suddenly felt a warm sensation wash over him. He looked at his hands, arms, and legs; they all glowed with a soft blue light. He said, "I'm ready!"

Tom got on Sage behind Oriana, holding on tight.

Emilie shouted, "Have fun, Tom! Don't worry, Oriana will take care of you. See you soon!"

He waved goodbye, and they headed out to sea.

A few minutes later, they picked up speed. Oriana said, "We are going to dive underwater. Don't be alarmed, Emilie's magic will protect you."

He nodded. Sage jumped in the air and dove straight down. Tom didn't feel a thing when they went underwater. They dove deeper and deeper into the sea. A few minutes later, they reached the seabed, and an array of bright, iridescent colors came into view. Brilliant pinks, purples, and blues illuminated the waters surrounding them. There were massive coral reefs, and a multitude of colorful fish swam by. Tom was amazed by the beauty in front of him.

Oriana got off Sage, swam alongside him, and said, "Welcome to Meridien."

There were large schools of fish that shifted as one into different shapes. The friendly blue dolphins passed by and said hello to Tom. They passed a cluster of twenty giant clamshells. Most of the clamshells were open, but six of them were closed.

Oriana said, "This is where the mermaids sleep."

One of the clamshells opened, and out came a mermaid who swam toward Oriana.

Oriana said, "Hello, Aria. Have a good rest?"

Aria said, "Yes, I had a good nap. I'm going to the shore to say hello. See you guys there!"

Oriana said, "See you on top."

Tom said, "This is where you sleep? This is your home? I thought it would be something like Atlantis or an underwater city where you would gather at."

Oriana said, "Atlantis? What is a city?"

Tom said, "A city has buildings and freeways or waterways where you travel on. I guess not. It's Hollywood's take on Meridien."

Oriana said, "Hollywood?"

Tom said, "Never mind, I mean, I was expecting more of a place with tall buildings and guards with pitchforks at the entrance to your city. Do you have a palace and throne where you sit and rule Meridien?"

Oriana laughed and said, "A palace and throne? What would we do with buildings or guards? We have no need for these things. Meridian is beautiful as it is. You humans have very wild imaginations."

They swam farther and saw many other clusters of giant clamshells.

Tom said, "How many mermaids live here? And how long has Meridien existed?"

Oriana said, "There are a couple thousand of us, and we've been around for about ten thousand years."

Tom said, "That long?" He thought for a moment and continued, "You know, where I'm from, mermaids are mythical creatures that don't exist. You exist only in folklore or stories. I think perhaps a visitor came back to Earth and wrote about you and other creatures like dragons and unicorns. I mean, you've existed way before mankind, and the resemblance and descriptions in storybooks are almost exact. Was one of the past visitors a writer?"

Oriana said, "Hmmm, that is interesting, and it would explain how human visitors know about us. I'm not sure if there was a writer, but you may want to ask Theodore. He would be the one who is most knowledgeable about the subject. You know, he is quite the clever owl. He was the one that gave us our name ten thousand years ago."

Tom said, "Theodore named you? What do you mean?"

Oriana said, "We originally were known as the Meridian maidens. Theodore said that Meridian maidens was just too long of a name, so he shortened it, taking the first three letters of *Meridian* and the first four letters of *maidens*, and called us *mermaids* for short. Brilliant idea, right? Ever since then, we've been known as mermaids."

Tom said, "Ah, I see. So Theodore came up with the name 'mermaid.' That is very clever."

They continued to explore the underwater world and came to what looked like a huge bed of pink, purple, and turquoise flowers. As they got closer, Tom noticed something different. He said, "I can smell something, something like flowers? But here in the water?"

Oriana said, "Yes, these are Meridien flowers. They are all over Meridien growing in big cluster beds like these."

Tom said, "I can't believe it smells like flowers on the bottom of the sea. Who would have known?"

Oriana said, "Well, Tom, it's getting late, we better head to shore."

Sage propelled upward. Minutes later, they were at the surface and headed toward the beach.

Oriana said, "You know, I've been meaning to ask you something. Why do humans throw their garbage anywhere they please? We've had visitors in the past leaving their trash and unwanted items anywhere they like, even throwing garbage in our waterways that eventually lead to our beautiful sea, which is my home. Is this a common practice on Earth?"

Tom said, "Yes, unfortunately, trash in our waterways and oceans is very common. There are tons of garbage accumulating in our waters, and the majority of that is plastic pollution."

Oriana said, "What is plastic pollution?"

Tom said, "Pollution is where you introduce contaminants or dangerous things to natural environments, like trash in your sea waters. And plastic has been a human necessity for many years. We use plastic in many things, like bags, bottles, caps, and packaging material. The problem is that plastic is non-biodegradable, which means that it can't break down into natural materials. It's simply indestructible and carries toxins that spread among marine life. Millions of seabirds and marine animals die every year because they ingest the plastic or get entangled in it. It's also bad for us because we get chemical poisoning by eating these fish. They say there's enough plastic in the ocean to circle the Earth four times. It's a terrible thing, and it's just getting worse."

Oriana said, "This is very sad to hear. How has it come to this point? Is there something being done about this?"

Tom said, "Yes, there are organizations that are trying to reduce ocean plastic pollution, but we need to do more. We need to concentrate on third-world countries who are responsible for ninety-five percent of the plastic pollution in our oceans due to bad infrastructure and not having facilities to treat their waste. What's also a big concern is fishing nets that account for almost half of the pollution. Commercial fishermen just leave or dispose their nets in the water, and they trap and kill these poor animals. Governments need to take more responsibility and enforce global regulations to deal with these factors. We also need to take personal responsibility and reduce our use of plastic."

Oriana said, "It seems you know how to help these poor animals and you care what happens to them. I'm sure that there are other people that care like you and share the same views. Perhaps together you can stop this pollution and save creatures like us in your world."

Tom sighed and said, "It would take many people and governments to work together to solve a problem of this magnitude. But I really would like to see our oceans free of pollution like it is here in Meridien. Perhaps one day it will happen."

They reached the shores of Azar, and Oriana said, "I hope you enjoyed your tour of Meridien."

Tom said, "I did enjoy it. Thank you both for the tour."

Oriana said, "I will see you again in a couple days to take you back to the portal. Please think about our discussion earlier."

Tom said, "I will."

It was time to head home. They all said goodbye to the sea creatures and flew back to the Enchanted Forest.

DAY 7
THE ENLIGHTENMENT

TOM AWOKE BRIGHT AND EARLY AND WAS ESPE-cially excited, as today, they were going to see the Great Owl himself—Theodore. Theodore lived in the Emerald Forest, which was a distance away, so an early start was necessary. Tom was also in good spirits this morning because in two days, he was going home. He looked forward to sleeping in his own bed, eating a hearty meal, and seeing his family. He promised himself the first thing he would do would be to take a trip to see his mother. Her birthday was coming up, and she would definitely love a surprise visit.

Everyone gathered outside and had breakfast at the table.

Emilie said, "We've got to hurry up. We need to make a stop on the way."

Tom said, "I thought we were going to spend the day at Theodore's. Are we seeing anyone else?"

Cody said, "Yup, we'll make a quick stop to see my family. My grandpa George just arrived, and I want to say hello."

They quickly finished breakfast and flew north toward Emerald Forest.

The first stop was Rainbow Valley, where they'd land and continue on foot. Thirty minutes elapsed, and Tom saw a cluster of rainbows up ahead. He shouted, "I see it, Rainbow Valley, it's coming up!"

They landed atop a grassy hill where hundreds of rainbows surrounded them.

Tom looked up and said, "Hey, Cody, look at you, you're under a double rainbow. You see the rainbow above you? The outer arc is red, and the inner arc is violet. Now, look above that, it's a rainbow with the colors reversed—the outer arc is violet, and the inner arc is red. That is a double rainbow, my friend. I haven't seen that before."

Nala said, "Tom, you should see the one you're standing under, looks like a double-double rainbow to me."

They all turned and looked up, and indeed, it was a double-double rainbow with the colors reversed on each arc—four of them stacked on top each other.

Tom said, "It would be called a quadruple rainbow, Nala. Double-double is the name of a famous burger back home. I wouldn't mind having a couple of those right now. And a vanilla shake, of course." Tom laughed and licked his lips.

They continued north, exiting Rainbow Valley, and stopped at a river to quench their thirst. Tom splashed his face with water, looked up, and saw something large and metallic shining behind the trees. He said to Nala, "What is that shinning behind the trees over there?"

Nala gulped down the water, looked up, and casually said, "It's a spaceship."

Tom exclaimed, "What?! A spaceship, like, from outer space?"

Nala took another drink and nonchalantly said, "Yup."

Tom quickly walked through the shallow water and ran toward the metal object.

Emilie yelled out, "Where are you going?!"

Tom ran as fast as he could. He thought, *This must belong to the aliens that Emilie was speaking about.*

Panting and out of breath, he reached the object and stared in awe. It was a large metallic, silver spaceship that stood forty feet high and seventy feet wide. It was disc-shaped and made of burnished metal. No windows, doors, or entranceways were visible; the entire structure was solid as a rock. There were also no markings or flags of countries to claim it. *It has to be from an alien nation,* he thought. He gazed in amazement at this giant piece of metal.

Emilie, Nala, and Cody arrived, and Tom asked, "How long has this been here?"

Emilie said, "For about five hundred years. It was left here as a gift to Azar by Anthara from Nexium. Nexium is a planet in the Andromeda galaxy next to yours. And, yes, it is what you humans would refer to as an 'alien' spaceship. Anthara had gone through the portal and crashed right here by the trees. Theodore was captivated by the spaceship, so Anthara gave it to Azar as a token of his appreciation for our hospitality. Honestly, Tom, I don't know what your fascination is about 'aliens.' They are just like you and me—well, they do look kinda different in a ghoulish way, but so do some of the creatures here on Azar."

They all laughed.

"We've had about three alien visitors, and all of them were well-mannered, kind, and very, very intelligent creatures," Emilie continued, "way more advanced in technology than you humans are. I mean, all those gadgets inside this spaceship, Theodore was fascinated. They would spend a lot of time at Theodore's home sharing data they had gathered from their visits to other planets and galaxies. Each of them was a wealth of information. In fact, I'm sure you and Anthara would get along perfectly!"

Tom said doubtfully, "Really? Hmm, well, I don't know about that. Can I go inside it?"

Emilie said, "No. No one is allowed inside except Theodore. But we must continue on if we are to make it in time to see him."

Tom nodded and gazed one last time at the beautiful piece of alien art.

They walked up a mountain and reached a plateau that overlooked valleys of beautiful red rock formations. A large river zig-zagged through the valleys, and the sound of rushing water could be heard from atop the plateau.

Cody said, "We'll need to fly over there where my parents are waiting."

Tom got on Cody's back, and they all flew toward the farthest plateau.

Tom saw two dragons hovering in the sky. He said, "I think I see your parents, is that them up ahead?"

Cody said, "No, they're not my parents, they're my cousins."

Seconds later, a dozen dragons came into view. Tom said to Cody, "Umm, remember earlier when you said I'll meet your family? How many dragons are we talking about, Cody?"

They ascended higher and higher till they had flown over the tallest peak, and the sky opened up to hundreds of dragons soaring through the skies.

"Wow!" Tom said in amazement.

Cody said, "Welcome to Dragonia, Tom."

Tom said, "Dragonia—what a sight!"

They landed near the river and were greeted by Cody's parents, Georgina and Archie.

Cody said, "Tom, this is Georgina, my mom, and Archie, my father."

Tom said, "Nice to meet you both."

Archie said, "Welcome to Dragonia, Tom. We've heard a lot about you. I hope our Cody is taking good care of you?"

Tom said, "Yes, of course. Cody, Emilie, and Nala take excellent care of me."

Georgina said, "You must all be famished after the journey. Let's go to Aunt Ester's place to have some refreshments."

They followed Georgina and Archie up a hill to a large grassy area. Tom spotted three baby dragons playing hide-and-seek behind some trees. The baby dragons saw Tom, ran up to him, and stared curiously at the visitor. They were each differently colored. One was red, one was blue, and one was green. They were very cute creatures that stood seven feet tall, each with a long, scaly tail that wagged back and forth. They had big black eyes with long, curly eyelashes, and when they smiled, two large front teeth protruded. The baby dragons had oversized hands and feet and a line of scaly horn-like spikes that ran down the backs of their heads all the way to the tips of their tails. They had large angel-like wings that rested on their sides. They stared at Tom in amazement, wondering what this human was doing in Dragonia.

The baby green dragon stepped forward and said, "My name is Jimmy Dragon, but you can call me Jimmy D."

The baby blue dragon stepped forward and said, "My name is Winston Dragon, but you can call me Winston D."

The baby red dragon stepped forward and said, "And my name is Draco Dragon, but you can just call me Draco for short!"

All three baby dragons looked at Tom, smiled, wagged their tails, and looked absolutely adorable.

Tom said, "My name is Tom. Nice to meet you all."

A red female dragon came up behind them and said, "Let's not be rude and stare at the visitor, little ones. Now run along and play."

The babies smiled, waved goodbye to Tom, and ran off to continue their game of hide-and-seek. The red female dragon gave Cody, Emilie, and Nala big hugs. She then turned to Tom and said, "Hello, there. You must be Tom. My name is Aunt Ester. Sorry about the little ones, but we rarely see humans here in Dragonia. Please come and meet the family."

There were dozens of dragons having a picnic and talking amongst themselves. Tom saw a green male dragon sitting in a chair eating pie; he looked like an older version of Cody.

They stopped in front of the green dragon, and Georgina said, "Tom, I would like you to meet my father, George. He's visiting from Dragonia."

Tom said, "Hello, nice to meet you. You're visiting from Dragonia? I'm confused—isn't this Dragonia?"

George laughed. "I'm visiting from Dragonia the planet. This here is Dragonia Two, but we just call it Dragonia for short."

Tom, surprised, asked, "Dragonia the planet? There is a planet of dragons?"

George said, "Yes, there is! It's mostly inhabited by dragons, but there are also some dinosaurs that roam the lands."

Tom said, "Dinosaurs?! Alive?"

George laughed again and said, "Yes, you seem surprised."

Tom said, "Dinosaurs are extinct on Earth. They haven't existed for about twenty-three million years. And they exist on your planet?"

George said, "The majority of them exist on another planet in our solar system, Sepia. Sepia has about a million of them roaming the land. It's really quite a sight, but you won't want to go there, or you'll be stepped on!"

Everyone laughed.

Tom said, "Well, I definitely wouldn't want to be stepped on. Are there other planets out there?"

George said, "Yes, there are other planets in our solar system. But the best person to ask would be Theodore, he would be the most knowledgeable about the subject. You are to visit him next right?"

Tom said, "Yes, I'll add this to my list of questions."

"How about I take you on a quick tour of Dragonia…Two? That is, if it's okay with Cody here."

Cody said, "Be my guest, Grandpa George, the babies want me to teach them some air-maneuver tricks."

Tom and George took off and flew the skies of Dragonia. It was a vast, beautiful sight with many dragons roaming the land. There were magnificent, tall waterfalls, mountains, and breathtakingly beautiful landscapes of red rock formations. Tom could see Cody in the distance teaching the baby dragons mini loops and spins in the air.

Tom asked George, "How long did it take you to fly here from Dragonia the planet?"

George said, "Ah, well, it would take one day to fly here from Dragonia the planet, but we have other means of transportation that's much quicker. We walk through doors—when they are open, that is."

"What do you mean, walk through doors?"

George continued, "They are similar to the portal you came through from Earth to Azar but without all the hoopla involved. We just walk through, and here we are. But they only open at certain times. The Great Owls tell us where and when a door opens."

Tom made a mental note to ask Theodore about the "doors" to other planets.

George continued, "We better get you back if you want to be on time for Theodore, and we're just in time, as the babies are performing on stage."

They landed in an amphitheater-like open area where many dragons were gathered around a large stage.

George said, "The babies are gonna perform their new song 'The Dragon Groove.' Those littles ones are mighty talented. Come on, let's go to the front where Cody's at."

Tom and George walked to where Cody stood with Emilie and Nala. The baby dragons were lined up, and Jimmy Dragon took center stage. The crowd fell silent.

Jimmy grabbed the microphone and said, "Okay, ready Dragonia? Here we go now… Baby dragons, bust the beat."

Draco Dragon scratched on vinyl records, and Winston Dragon started to beatbox. The Dragonians went wild, waving their hands and dancing to the beat.

Jimmy Dragon rapped:

"Hey, all you funky dragons out there
Throw your hands up, and wave them in the air.
I'm the baby green dragon, and my name is Jimmy D
I'm the best baby rapper of the Dragon family."

"Now check this out:
Dilli bee bop a hoppin'
We're down right a rockin'
To this funky beat
Come on, Dragonia, get up on your feet!

Now listen carefully, and follow my instructions
I was taught by Sammy Mushroom of the Mushroom
Band Productions
So keepa walkin' tik tockin' to this hip-hop move
Come on, Azarians, let's do the Dragon Groove:

And do the fist pump
With both hands, now jump

Do the jiggy walk two times and stop

And do the jiggy walk two times, now pop

Half turn to the left, full turn to the right

Come on, Dragonia, let's party all night!"

"One…more…time…. The Dragon Groove!

And do the fist pump

With both hands, and jump

Do the jiggy walk two times and stop

And do the jiggy walk two times, now pop

Come on, Dragonia—throw down, don't stop!"

"Check this out….

We're gonna rock the night till the morning light

Hippa hoppin' tippa toppin' all the way past midnight.

Now remember me—my name is Jimmy D

I'm the best baby rapper of the Dragon family.

And tonight is the night we're gonna bring this house down.

We're the cute baby dragons, flying high, we're star-bound."

All three dragons pointed to the sky. Jimmy D continued to rap.

"Yeah, baby dragons! That's right, we're star-bound! Dance on, Dragonia!"

The dragons continued to dance the Dragon Groove and freestyle. The song ended, and dragons cheered and showed their excitement by breathing fire into the air. The baby dragons took a bow.

It was time to leave Dragonia. Tom said to the baby dragons, "You guys were great!" He thanked George for the tour and the Dragon family for their hospitality. Cody said goodbye to Georgina, Archie, and Grandpa George, and they flew off to Emerald Forest, where the Great Owl awaited.

They reached the edge of Emerald Forest and walked on a trail filled with a lush landscape of tropical plants and greenery. It was similar to the Enchanted Forest, but there were many more trees and a plentitude of brilliant, large green stones that appeared along the path.

Tom asked, "Are these green stones emeralds?"

Emilie said, "Yes, they are all over the forest; hence, the name

Emerald Forest."

As they walked deeper into the forest, the clouds rolled in, and the sky turned from blue to an eerie dark gray. Tom looked up into the trees and was spooked by the many owls silently watching his every move.

"We're here," Emilie said, as they stepped into a clearing and were faced by a wall of giant oak trees. Hundreds of owls were perched on the branches of the trees. "Theodore's tree is the one in the middle. You'll need to stand in front of it, Tom."

The oak tree was massive, as it stood one hundred feet tall and had a diameter of thirty feet. It was one of the biggest oak trees Tom had ever seen. The oak trees surrounding it were also large, but Theodore's was different, as there was much activity going on within it. Spread out over the trunk were a dozen small wooden doors, which owls entered and exited freely. Three larger doors were on the bottom of the trunk near the roots.

Tom stood in front of the big oak, and suddenly, hundreds of owls flew to the tree and covered every part of it. The owls hooted and screeched at high decibels, whistled, chirped, screamed, barked, and growled all at once. It was an excruciating sound, and

Tom covered his ears in pain. Seconds later, the tumultuous sounds of the owls stopped.

Tom uncovered his ears, shook his head, and looked up. A ghostly face of an owl had appeared on the trunk. It was a frightening sight, as the owl stared straight at Tom with its dark, fathomless black eyes that sent chills down his spine. The owl looked at everyone standing in front of it, then looked at Tom again and started to growl louder and louder.

In a deep, sinister voice, it shouted, "Who are you, and what is your purpose here?!"

Tom stepped forward and firmly said, "I am here to see Theodore. My name is Tom, and he is expecting me."

The owl stared at Tom with his cold, fathomless eyes, snickered, and shouted, "Well, then, wait here, human! I will inform the Great Owl you are here!" The face faded and disappeared from the tree trunk.

Seconds later, the owl's face reappeared and said, "Very well, he is expecting you. You may all enter through the bottom door on your right." The face disappeared again.

Tom looked at the door they were to enter and said, "How will I fit through that door? It's too small."

Emilie said, "Looks can be deceiving. This is a magical door. Cody, you go first."

Tom laughed and said, "Cody, fit through that door? Impossible!"

Cody stepped to the door and said, "Watch this." He stuck his finger in the door and got pulled in little by little. His finger, hand, head, body, and then his tail were sucked in piece by piece. And—*Boom!*—Cody was in the tree.

Cody yelled from inside, "See, Tom, it sucks you in. You'll just feel a little tickle, but don't worry, everything will fit."

Tom stared in disbelief as Nala went next. Nala said, "Watch this, I'll go in tail first." Nala stuck his tail in the door and got sucked in little by little. First went his tail, then feet, then body, and then paws, and—*Boom!*—Nala was in the tree.

Nala laughed and said, "Your turn, Tom."

Tom immediately went to the door, stuck his hand in the doorway, and felt a tug and then a stronger tug. He felt his entire body being stretched and pulled. He felt a tickle and—*Boom!*—he was magically in the tree.

Emilie quickly followed, and they all stood in the entranceway of Theodore's home, which was nothing like the outside of the tree; it was completely astounding.

The entranceway was very impressive, with towering ceilings and walls made of an opalescent, pearly rock material similar to moonstone. It possessed a magical color that shifted from white to silver to blue and then to rainbow, which glowed and made the walls and ceiling seem to move. In the middle of the room was a large table of books.

Theodore walked in the room and said, "Hello, my friends! Welcome to my humble abode."

Theodore was dressed in a smart blue jacket, wore gold-rimmed spectacles, and held a brown leather-bound book in his hand titled *Astronomy*. He was followed by two young owls dressed in school uniforms. They held the same book of astronomy that Theodore carried. They wore blue blazers with a patch on the lapel that had the letters "G" and "O" intertwined in gold threading. The "G" and "O" insignia stood for the school of the "Great Owls."

Theodore said, "These are two of my newest students who are studying to be Great Owls one day. Now, run along, boys, and we will continue the lesson tomorrow."

The students obediently nodded and flew away.

Theodore turned to everyone and said, "Tom, you will come with me? I would like to show you my school of the Great Owls. Emilie, Nala, and Cody, I have some refreshments set up for you in the garden, and Tom and I will be out shortly."

Emilie, Nala, and Cody headed toward the garden.

Theodore looked at Tom for a moment and said, "My, my, I can see that you have many questions on your mind, and I will answer all of them. But now let us take a tour of the school."

Theodore walked to the next room, and Tom followed. The second room was a gigantic library full of books neatly stacked on shelves that spanned from the floor to the massive ceiling and seemed endless.

Theodore said, "Give me a minute, Tom. I need to put this book away." He flew up to the fiftieth row, placed the book on a shelf, then flew down.

Tom asked, "I've never seen so many books in one room. This must be the tallest library that exists. I can't even see where it ends up there."

Theodore said, "Well, yes, you would need wings to see how high it goes." Theodore winked. "This library is seven hundred feet tall, and it's stacked all the way to the top. I do love books, and this is a collection of different subjects curated over hundreds and thousands of years. In fact, we are running out of space and will need to create a second library soon. Come, let us continue on."

Tom followed Theodore into an enormous room where different picture screens of planets, moons, stars, and galaxies were displayed in real time on the walls and up on the ceiling. Tom was absolutely delighted, as it felt as if he had just stepped into outer space and was walking amongst the stars.

Theodore said, "This is our space observatory. This is where we study the stars, planets, galaxies, and any other objects in outer space. It's how we know when the portal will open and many other phenomena that occur not only on Azar but on other planets in our solar system and beyond. Let us join my students at that diagram over there."

They walked to the other side of the room where ten students stood with a Great Owl. The Great Owl spoke as the students took notes and asked questions.

Theodore said to Tom, "This side of the room is made up of different sections of our galaxy, which is called the Utopian Galaxy. I will show you how we predict when the portal will open over Azar. The picture directly above us was taken from our skies last night. That star there is called the Star of Azar. It is the biggest and brightest star in our skies. It is similar to your Polaris, or North Star, you see on Earth. Do you see the seven stars around the Star of Azar that make a V shape? Do you see it, Tom?"

Tom nodded and said, "Yes, I see it."

Theodore continued, "They are known as an asterism, or a distinctive group of stars like Earth's Little Dipper. Now, listen carefully. The V is supposed to be an L. If you look closely, you'll see it is almost a perfectly shaped V. When it becomes a perfect V, the porthole opens to the other worlds. It will be a perfect V in two days when it is your time to go back home. Then the stars will realign again and form back into an L shape. But I'm afraid there is not just this porthole that we must worry about, but two others that have recently opened up on other planets in our solar system."

Tom said, "There are other portholes?"

Theodore nodded and said, "Yes, I'm afraid so. Seven years ago, on the planet of Sepia, a human went through the porthole and was accidentally stepped on by a dinosaur. Horrible scene, as he was flattened like a pancake! And just a year ago, another porthole opened on the planet of Dragonia during their fire-breathing contest. Well, we all know what happened to him. The poor little human was in the wrong place at the wrong time and was fried to a crisp. It was not our fault, really. This is why we must study the stars to predict when and where a porthole will open just like I do here. I mean, I cannot be in three places at the same time, and who knows how many more portholes are out there?"

Tom said, "Ah, that was what Grandpa George was talking about. I thought he was joking, but he was serious about being 'stepped on' if I were to go to Sepia. So it actually happened to a human. He also mentioned doors that you walk through to get to other planets."

Theodore said, "Yes, that is correct. Great Owls are adept at finding doors, as we can actually see them. They tend to move around depending on the time of year, but they are easy to find, and we make note of them and let other creatures know when and where to enter them. We can only travel through doors to planets in our solar system, not to all of them. And speaking of planets, let us walk to the picture at the far end."

They stood in front of a diagram of a solar system. Theodore said, "This is Azar's solar system. You see, this is our sun, and here are the planets that revolve around the sun. We have seven different planets in our solar system. Azar, Dragonia, Sepia, Navia, Zvikonia, Utopia, and Dystopia, which is our newest planet."

Tom laughed and said, "Dystopia? Is that where all the bad creatures go?"

Theodore said, "Yes. In fact, it was recently created not for bad creatures but for very bad humans."

"Humans?" Tom thought for a minute and said, "Is this where the poacher is? He's in Dystopia?"

Theodore smiled and said, "That is correct, him and a few others that were 'problems.' It was not my doing, oh no. In circumstances like these, it is the decision of a higher level—our Queen, our creator. She created in one day the planet Dystopia for 'problems.' The poacher was placed there and only lasted for a few hours… stepped right into the serpent's mouth!"

Tom asked in confusion , "You have a Queen, a creator? She created a planet in one day?"

Theodore said, "Yes, she is our creator, the creator of Azar, the planets, the galaxies, and your galaxy, your planet Earth. But you must remember, our Queen creates, she does not destroy. That is left to us Azarians and you humans. And that brings us to why you are standing in front of me today. You see, Tom, you were chosen. You came through the portal not by chance but by purpose. Our Queen is very concerned about the problems that are happening on Earth. We believe you can help make a difference and change your world into a better place…with a little help from us, that is."

Tom was taken aback. "I was chosen? This can't be true. Is this a joke?"

Theodore took a deep breath and said, "Follow me, I would like to show you something."

Theodore walked down a hall and entered his study. It was a grand room that had dark wooden, coffered high ceilings and paneled walls. The furnishings were each meticulously carved from a lustrous dark brown wood. There was a large desk and two oversized chairs that sat opposite a picture window, which looked out to the garden. Tom looked out the window and saw Emilie, Nala, and Cody having tea and cakes.

Theodore waved Tom over to the desk. In front of Theodore stood his magic crystal ball. It was a large crystal ball that was two feet in diameter and rested on a wooden pedestal. Tom saw clouds hovering inside of it.

Theodore said, "Take a look at the ball, and tell me what you see."

Tom looked closely and saw an ocean filled with trash and plastic bottles floating on the surface. There was a seal sticking his head out of the water trying to swim away from the tons of trash that surrounded it. The picture disappeared, and another picture surfaced of a baby elephant standing next to its mother that lay down on the ground bleeding with her ivory tusks missing. The image faded out, and another scene appeared of a fire raging through a forest. Animals were desperately running from the blazes. Homes were burning, and people were frantic. There was chaos everywhere.

Tom looked at Theodore and said, "This is heartbreaking."

Theodore nodded, and Tom looked at the magic ball as the tragic scene disappeared. Another image appeared of a beautiful beach with homes scattered across the high cliffs.

Tom smiled and said, "This is Malibu, where I live."

The image of the beautiful houses suddenly filled with flames. Fire was everywhere, ravaging homes. There was widespread destruction that caused havoc amongst the people.

Tom was shocked and upset. He shook his head and sadly said, "Why are you showing me this, Theodore?"

Theodore said, "Because humans are on the path to destruction! And the queen is very upset!"

Tom said, "What? The queen is upset? What does all this have to do with me?"

Theodore said, "I know this all comes as a shock to you, but I will explain to you how all this will come together. Please, have a seat."

Tom sat on the other side of the desk and listened intently.

Theodore continued, "Our queen created Earth for you humans. She provided the human race with everything that was needed— food, water, land—the basic essentials needed to survive. She gave you intelligence and imagination that led to the creation of wonderful inventions to further the evolution of the human race. But something happened—the human race went from good to bad to worse. There has been a total disregard of Earth's natural habitat and a disregard to its inhabitants both human and animal. The queen will not take any more of this irresponsible behavior—she is very upset! In fact, I've never seen her so angry, and frankly, it scares me!"

Theodore paused for a moment then said, "And this is where you come in, Tom. You will need to start the process to mend what has already been done in order to avoid future destruction."

Tom was overwhelmed with emotion. He sat back in his chair, took a deep breath, and sighed loudly. "I am just one person. I've been saying this to all you Azarians—what can one person do?"

Theodore said, "It was one person who created electricity and one person who created a car and a computer. Two brothers invented the first airplane that changed your entire world. It started with a simple thought, Tom, a thought that turned into reality."

Theodore paused and continued, "There is a bright side to all of this. You humans still have an opportunity to shape what lies ahead, and it will start with you, Tom, and people who have the same morals and values that you do. But I must warn you, if things do not change on Earth now, the destruction of Earth and the human race is imminent. What happens in the future is really up to you humans. So I will leave you with this thought, Tom. Think about the problems that are going on in your world, use your imagination on how to deal with these issues, and this is how things will start to change for the better. And, also, I need to ask of you an important favor."

Tom said, "Yes, what is it?"

Theodore took something out of his top desk drawer and handed Tom a beautiful emerald that was two inches in length. "This is a special stone. It is an emerald from my forest. I need you to take this with you through the portal. If it ends up on the other side with you, an Azarian might be able to come to Earth. And if that is the case, it would be another story to write, won't it?" Theodore winked at Tom.

Tom smiled and said, "Sure, of course. But what do I do with it?"

Theodore said, "Keep the emerald in a safe place next to you. It will help you on your journey through life…to your destiny."

Tom took it and looked at the beautiful light that was emanating from the stone. He turned to Theodore and said, "This is a magic stone, isn't it? Will it turn into a creature? Never mind, I don't want to know." Tom placed the emerald in his pocket and said, "I'm ready to go back home."

They joined the others in the garden and talked about the next day's festivities. The Festival of Azar was the biggest event of the year.

Theodore said, "Tom, you're in for a real treat. Jane Peacock and our very own Cody will perform a duet that is marvelous! In fact, speaking of Jane Peacock, I must get going. I need to pick up my jacket and prepare for tomorrow's festivities. I wouldn't want to be late for Jane, or she'll bite my head off!"

Everyone laughed, and Emilie said, "We must get going, too. Harry dropped off our outfits for the festival, including a couple suits for you to try on, Tom."

Tom thanked Theodore for his hospitality, and they all flew off to the Enchanted Forest.

DAY 8
THE FESTIVAL OF AZAR

THE TRUMPETERS RAISED THEIR HORNS AND SOUNDED off that the festivities had begun. The Azarians came in their finest attire, dressed to impress. Cody, Georgina, and Archie manned the refreshment booth with plenty of dragon beer, exotic drinks, and Azar's favorite delicacies. The Wuzzlies rolled in and bounced to the rhythm of the beat. Bakari pranced in with his fellow emperor and empress cats. They walked up to Tom and belted out a big *ROAR!* that shook the whole dance floor, and everyone laughed. Nala, Emilie, and the baby dragons were doing the famous "Jiggy Walk" moves while Grandpa George watched and enjoyed a big mug of dragon beer. On the grandstand in center stage was The Mushroom Band decked out in tailored tuxes, and Sammy the Mushroom looked as chic as ever as they played the Azarians' favorite tunes.

Then Theodore came on stage, and everyone was silent. He said, "Welcome, fellow Azarians, to the Festival of Azar! I hope you all are having a grand old time! I would also like to welcome our special guest, Tom, whom I'm sure you've all met. As you know, Tom will be leaving us tomorrow and going back to his world on Earth. From his world, we Azarians have enjoyed the many gifts that have been bestowed upon us from our human visitors. By gifts, I mean music, song, and dance—just to name a few. But we are especially grateful for one gift in particular, and that is opera. In honor of your departure tomorrow, Tom, we would like to perform for you a song that is dear to us Azarians. Without further ado, may I present our very own Cody and Jane Peacock, performing one of our favorite opera tunes!"

Everyone clapped and whistled as the curtains were drawn. The Mushroom Band orchestra played joyful music as Cody walked on stage dressed in a black tux jacket with a white tie. He placed his hands on his tuxedo lapels, stood proudly, then belted out beautiful long notes in Italian. Jane Peacock walked on stage and countered with stunning, bold soprano tones as the Azarians swayed to the upbeat tune. Creatures sat at tables and held their glasses up high as they sang along. Cody and Jane Peacock sang the final verses and finished with a brilliant, strong note. Everyone clapped, whistled, and shouted with joy.

Cody and Jane Peacock bowed, and the crowd gave a standing

ovation. Theodore came on stage and thanked them for an outstanding performance. The Mushroom Band continued to play the Azarians' favorite songs throughout the night.

It was getting late and eventually was time to leave. Tom thanked and said goodbye to each Azarian. He said to Theodore, "Thank you for everything, Theodore. I will make Azar proud."

Theodore said, "I know you will, Tom. We'll be keeping an eye on you!"

Tom, Emilie, Nala, and Cody quietly took off to the Enchanted Forest to prepare for the big day tomorrow.

DAY 9
THE DEPARTURE

TOM BARELY SLEPT, AS HE WAS SO EXCITED TO GO home. An early breakfast was served with his favorite food—flapjacks soaked in syrup and a pitcher of his favorite drink, the Dragon's Delight. They quickly finished breakfast and flew toward the waters of Azar. They landed on the white sand beaches, and Oriana the Mermaid and Sage the Seahorse stood ready to take him to the portal.

Tom walked to the shore and turned to Emilie, Nala, and Cody. "Aren't you guys coming?"

Emilie sadly said, "No, Tom, I think it's better if we stay here." She ran up to him and gave him a hug.

Nala walked to Tom and affectionately rubbed alongside him while Tom rubbed Nala's head and said goodbye.

Tom went up to Cody and said, "I'm going to miss flying with you, Cody."

Cody nodded sadly and gave him a hug.

Tom slowly walked to the shore, turned around, and said to them, "I will miss all of you, my dear friends."

He got on Sage, hung onto Oriana, and rode off one last time into the beautiful turquoise waters of Azar.

10 YEARS LATER

Emilie, Nala, and Cody sat in Theodore's garden having tea.

Theodore came out to the garden and said, "It's time."

They all went into Theodore's study and gathered in front of the magic crystal ball. Clouds circled within it before an image appeared of Tom on the news surrounded by many people at the beach. He stood in front of the TV cameras and spoke to the reporter. A news ticker appeared on the bottom that said, "Tom Jamison—Philanthropist donating millions to the clean-up of the world's oceans."

Theodore looked at everyone and smiled. The image disappeared, and another picture appeared. Tom was standing in the Amazon rainforest. He was on the news speaking to a reporter when a news ticker appeared on the screen. It said, "Tom Jamison, president of *United World Wildlife Foundation,* starts nine new sanctuaries located in Africa and Asia and speaks out against deforestation to save our planet."

The picture disappeared, and another image of Tom appeared. He was standing in Copenhagen's city center speaking to a reporter and surrounded by people. A news ticker came on the screen that said, "Tom Jamison, with the help of other celebrity philanthropists, donated 100 million dollars to fund projects in cities around the world, like Copenhagen, to 'Go Green and Clean.' The fund supports cities to be eco-friendly and carbon neutral and to reduce carbon emissions for a cleaner, healthier way of life for the world."

The picture disappeared, and a new image appeared of Tom sitting at his desk in his study. He got up and walked out the room. The crystal ball focused back on Tom's desk. The top drawer opened, and in it was a green stone that started to emanate a vibrant, beautiful green glow. It was the emerald from Theodore's forest. They all stared in awe at the crystal ball as the emerald's light grew stronger and stronger, lighting up the entire room.

Theodore looked at everyone and said mischievously, "Watch out, Earthlings, the Azarians are coming to town."

Everyone smiled with delight. Another image appeared of Tom walking into a room where a woman held a baby dressed in pink. The woman rocked the baby to sleep. Tom took the baby in his arms and smiled. He gave her a kiss on the head and gently laid her down in the crib. He said, "Sweet dreams, my little Emilie." The magic crystal ball went blank.

Emilie looked up at everyone with a tear in her eye. She smiled proudly and said, "He has a baby daughter…Emilie."

The End

GALLERY OF THE STARS

BAKARI THE EMPEROR CAT

NALA THE WHITE TIGER

DRACODIAN "CODY" DRAGON

EMILIE THE PIXIE

TOM

THEODORE

WUZZLY

JANE PEACOCK

BABY DRAGONS

THE ROSE TREES

WILLOW THE UNICORN

MERMAIDS OF MERIDIEN

ORIANA &
THE BLUE DOLPHINS

THE WONDERFUL SONGS OF AZAR

THE DRAGON GROOVE

"Hey, all you funky dragons out there
Throw your hands up, and wave them in the air.
I'm the baby green dragon, and my name is Jimmy D
I'm the best baby rapper of the Dragon family."

"Check this out:
Dilli bee bop a hoppin'
We're down right a rockin'
To this funky beat
Come on, Dragonia, get up on your feet!

Now listen carefully, and follow my instructions
was taught by Sammy Mushroom of the Mushroom Band Productions
So keepa walkin' tik tockin' to this hip-hop move
Come on, Azarians, let's do the Dragon Groove:

And do the fist pump
With both hands, now jump!

Do the jiggy walk two times and stop
And do the jiggy walk two times, now pop!

Half turn to the left, full turn to the right
Come on, Dragonia, let's party all night!"

"One…more…time…. The Dragon Groove!
And do the fist pump
With both hands, and jump
Do the jiggy walk two times and stop
And do the jiggy walk two times, now pop
Come on, Dragonia—throw down, don't stop!"

"Check this out….
We're gonna rock the night till the morning light
Hippa hoppin' tippa toppin' all the way past midnight.

Now remember me—my name is Jimmy D
I'm the best baby rapper of the Dragon family.
And tonight is the night we're gonna bring this house down.
We're the cute baby dragons, flying high, we're star-bound."

EMPERORS ROAR!!

"Here it comes, the Emperor's ROAR!,
Lo and behold, it's the Emperor's ROAR!

When Bakari commands, we stand and obey
He shouts, 'Bring out the liquid gold!'
Now stand aside and clear the way!

For here it comes, the Emperor's ROAR!
Lo and behold, it's the Emperor's ROAR!

A trickle of gold
A drop of delight
It's the drink to behold
At the end you just might

ROAR! at the top of your lungs
ROAR! The celebration has begun
ROAR! to the golden delight
It's the emperor's fruit that gleams in the light!

Here it comes, the Emperor's ROAR!,
All hail and behold, it's the Emperor's ROAR!

THE MOON DANCE

Now all you funky creatures out there
Throw your hands up, and wave them in the air
Listen to me and follow my instructions
My name is Sammy Mushroom of the Mushroom Band
Production.

Come on, everyone, now get on your feet
Do the Moon Dance, and dance to the beat.
Two steps to the left, two steps to the right
Do the funky walk and dance all night!

Now let's shimmy shimmy up and shimmy shimmy down
Do the touchdown all the way to the ground
Get on your head and spin yourself around
That's it, Azarians! Now let's take it to town!

FUZZY WUZZLY WIGGLE WAGGLE

"We are the Wuzzlies, we love to fool around.
We ziggle and zaggle
And giggle and gaggle
And figgle and faggle!
We're faster than light!
Rolling, big balls of white!
We're the Wuzzlies from Azar!

We are the Wuzzlies, we love to bounce around.
Now don't you forget
And watch where your step
Cuz you'll deeply regret
Stepping on a Wuzzly from Azar!

We are the Wuzzlies, we love to dance around.
So get on your feet
And dance to this beat
Cuz you're in for a treat!
We're the Wuzzlies from Azar!

We ziggle and zaggle
And giggle and gaggle
And figgle and faggle!
We run at top speed!
So if you see us, please heed!
We're the wonderful…Wuzzlies…from…Azaaar!"

THE THREE GOLDEN RULES OF AZAR

The Golden Rules

#1 Do not harm or eat the creatures.

#2 No Littering allowed.

#3 Destruction of vegetation and sea habitat is strictly prohibited.

"Violation of the above Three Golden Rules will result in severe punishment and may include death."